Leslie Ford

Murder is the Pay-Off

WILDSIDE PRESS

ONE

CONNIE MAYNARD stopped a moment at the foot of the stairs and returned the critical unsmiling survey of the girl standing there in the looking glass across the bank of great tawny-bronze chrysanthemums. The girl was tawny-bronze herself, like the chrysanthemums—her hair and her smooth sun-tanned skin—except that her eyes were yellow-green and her green taffeta off-the-shoulder dress clothed her with infinitely more art than chrysanthemum leaves ever have in mind. Constance Maynard regarded herself coolly there for a moment, then turned and crossed the hall into the library, the green taffeta swishing softly and with complete confidence as she moved. It was the least flattering mirror in the house, old, critical and prejudiced . . . like some of the people, Smithville's Finest, who would come swarming into the house in a few minutes now, eating and drinking their heads off— and covertly shaking them. The Prodigal Daughter . . . How long did you stay a returned prodigal in Smithville? It was six months now, going on seven, that Connie Maynard had been back home.

"Hi, Pops. All set?" She waited expectantly just inside the door for her father to turn and look at her. "What are you doing? Locking up the drinking whiskey?"

John Maynard, born in Kentucky, was big and slow and had never had occasion to hurry all parts of his body at the same time. He finished locking the cellarette and slipped the key into the pocket of his shabby dinner jacket.

"Now I wouldn't talk thataway, honey, if I was you." He drawled it amiably as he turned, smiling at his daughter. Women, horses, cards, guns or whiskey, none of them had ever surprised John Maynard out of his ordinary tempo or changed the slow smile on his extraordinary face. "Good God, Connie," he said equably, "you're nekkid as a jay-bird. Is that green rig a dress?"

"A dress? You mean *what* a dress, Daddy. Isn't it wonderful?"

She lifted her bare arms and whirled in a gay swishing circle for him to see. "This dress, Daddy, has design and purpose."

3

"Then I'd go take it off, Connie," John Maynard said. "He's not coming, for one thing."

Connie Maynard stopped abruptly, the laughter wiped instantly from her red lips and greenish eyes. "What do you mean, he's not coming?" she demanded sharply. "*Who's* not coming?"

"Gus Blake," her father drawled. He went over to the big mahogany desk cleared of everything except the green blotter and the silver ink-stand, and sat down on a corner of it. "Janey called up. They couldn't find a sitter."

"Oh, stuff!" She cut him off with a flippant swish of her taffeta bustle. "He'll come. So will Janey. Her mother always stays with the baby. It's just Janey's broken-wing tactics. They never work."

She was smiling and confident again. "Have we got a cigarette?" She took one from the box on the table beside her. "Janey's pretty stupid, Daddy. She just hasn't got any brains."

"And you have got 'em, honey?"

She looked at him quickly. His gentle drawl and the slow smile, easy and charming, that disguised the rugged lines of his massive face were snares she knew all about. She knew there was more she didn't know about him, but she did know that the slight stoop of his heavy shoulders was as conscious as the homely shabbiness of his dinner coat, and the black tie just enough askew to make men think he didn't much bother and women think he needed somebody to take care of him. A great big friendly brown dog, everybody's friend; John Maynard, slow and easy, simple as corn bread and pot likker, comfortable and unassuming and genial, with Smithville and Smith County and almost everybody in each, all neatly tied hand and foot securely in his inside vest pocket. "We ain't got much money, but we have a lot of fun . . ." John Maynard, who had more than plenty of money. The fullback with the Phi Beta Kappa key in the back of his desk drawer there. John Maynard, who'd drawled, "Communists? Well, I ain't much afraid of communists. When the ruckus died down I reckon I'd be Commissar of Smith County . . ."

She looked at him intently. "What do you mean, Dad? Of course I've got brains. You've told me so yourself."

"Then maybe you're not usin' 'em as well as you might," John Maynard said. "Been wantin' to talk to you about this. The purpose of brains, now, is to get you what you want out of life. You think it's Gus Blake you want."

The green eyes smoldered with sudden fire. "I know it's Gus Blake I want. He belongs to me. If I hadn't gone away he'd never have married!"

"Let's stick to facts, Connie. If you hadn't gone off and married that no-good ——"

"That was a mistake."

"I'm not criticizing you." He patted her shoulder gently. "You've had your fling. You've got your divorce and your own name back and the slate's clean. But Janey's got Gus. Now, wait a minute, Connie."

Connie Maynard stood rigidly beside the table, the color burning in her cheeks. "I'm waiting, Father."

"You came back home. You said you'd made a mistake. All right, honey, we all make mistakes. You said you'd found out it was Gus all the time and it was still Gus. You wanted him. You said if I'd give you a job on Gus's paper—let's just call it my paper—you'd get him back. And he didn't want you on the paper, but I sold him that one. I said you needed something to take your mind off yourself."

Connie Maynard moved impatiently. "Is this a cramming course in Ancient History I, Professor? I'm letter-perfect already.—You sound like Mother to me, Dad. She's on Janey's side too."

"I'm not on Janey's side. I'm on your side—right or wrong. I've always been on your side, honey. I don't say I approve, but you never asked me. I don't know as it's up to me to approve or disapprove. I expect there's a lot of things I do you don't approve of. But you're still on my side. Your mother's different. Your mother believes in ethics."

"What's ethics, Daddy?"

They both laughed. John Maynard's face sobered a little as he said, "It mightn't hurt either of us to try to find out what they are, sometime, honey."

"Sometime. Not right now, Daddy."

"Sometime when maybe somebody'll be tryin' to get Gus away from you? But that's not what I'm talkin' about, Connie. I'm sayin' I made Gus take you on the paper. And you've done well. I ain't sure but you could run the paper and me let Gus go. But that's not the point. The point is, Janey's still got Gus—and maybe you're bein' a little too obvious about what you want. That's not usin' your brains, Connie. That's what I don't like about that dress, for one thing. Gus ain't likely to fall for a nekkid woman——"

"I'm not naked, Daddy. And I'm tweed and high neck six days a week and this is relief. You can call it comic relief, but it's not."

"All right, all right. I'm just tryin' to help. I'm just tryin' to make you see maybe there's other ways of goin' about these things."

Her father's voice was mollifying and gentle.

"And I'm not saying I don't like Janey either. I do. I feel mighty sorry for Janey. She's a sweet little thing. She's just runnin' out of her class, is all. Gus is away out there, and so are you. Together the two of you can go places—big places. That's the sort of thing I like to see. Now wait, honey. Don't be impatient. Half of brains is the patience that comes along with 'em. You say Janey's stupid. You say she was off pickin' wild flowers the day brains were up for sale, and maybe you're right. But that's not the way to go about it, Connie. If you're dealin' with somebody stupid, honey, the thing to do is sit tight till they really do somethin' stupid. And I expect Janey's done it."

The bored detachment dropped from Connie Maynard like a drab shade falling from a naked light. She should have known her father better than to think he was lecturing her about a dress.

"What is it, Daddy? What's she done?"

"Got herself out on a limb," John Maynard said. His voice was soft and regretful. "Or I'm mighty afraid that's what she's gone and done. A mighty rickety limb at that. At least that's how it looks to me."

He reached back, unlocked the desk drawer and pulled it open. He took out a small oblong sheaf of papers and handed them over to his daughter.

"There's quite a pile of these things."

"Why, they're checks," Connie said. She turned them over in her hand. " 'Payable to the Smith County Recreation Company Inc.,' " she read. It was stamped on the back of each of them. She looked up at her father and back at the packet of checks. "Smith County Recreation Company," she repeated. "Isn't that your friend Doc Wernitz?"

She had a vague picture in her mind of the inconspicuous little man in a straight gray overcoat who'd come to the house a couple of times when his mechanics were all busy and reset the slot machine they had down in their play room in the basement. It was an old one he'd given her father on Christmas that had to be readjusted when the jackpot fell. She'd only noticed him because there was such a startling incongruity between his unobtrusive and self-effacing manner and the noisy clamor of the juke boxes and slot machines, labeled "Property of Smith County Recreation Company, Inc.," that he operated around the town.

"That's right. It's Doc Wernitz."

Her face was still blank as she turned the checks over and riffled through them. "They're all made out to the Sailing Club."

"And the Country Club. Ten dollars, mostly. A few twenties. That's the limit the clubs will cash."

"But that . . . that means *slot machines*?"

Her father nodded. She looked from him to the checks, still puzzled. One of them came loose from the staple that held them and floated down to the floor. She put her hand out to catch it.

"Don't worry, honey," John Maynard drawled. "It'll bounce."

Then Connie Maynard understood.

"Oh," she said. "Oh. They're rubber. They're all rubber."

"They're all rubber," her father said equably. "Three hundred and twenty dollars' worth. Not counting the bank's cleared something under a thousand dollars the last few months. Jim Ferguson gave these to me today at the directors' meeting. He don't know what to do about 'em. He likes Janey, and I expect he don't much like the idea of going to Gus about 'em."

"I don't blame him."

"Neither do I."

Connie looked down at the checks again. The clock on the mantel ticked on towards seven o'clock. Upstairs a door opened and closed. Her father put out his hand.

"I still don't get it, Dad," she said. "Look at these dates. Here's one to the Sailing Club on June 12th. This one's July 4th. It's November now. Why——"

"They were coming in too thick and fast, I expect. Doc Wernitz cashed a hundred or so a month and hung on to the rest. It's a deal the clubs have with him, honey. He usually cashes checks when the banks are closed and the clubs run out of silver—but he takes checks a lot of times if there's some question the clubs might have trouble collecting."

John Maynard shrugged. "He can collect without anybody's feelings getting hurt, or just write the loss off to public relations. Like Gus. If Doc Wernitz was sticking around Smithville he wouldn't want to antagonize the editor of the local paper. He's torn up a lot of checks in his time—influential people, and people he might scare into stopping play if they realized the hole they'd got themselves in. But he's pulling out of Smithville now, selling out and going south, so he don't care about editors and people with influence any more. I expect there'll be a lot of headaches in town tomorrow. Seems like it's powerful easy to write a check at the bar when you're playing the slot machines and forget to put it down when you get home with nothing to show for it. I bet Janey hasn't any idea of the amount that's out against her. That's why Ferguson let me take these this afternoon, to see if I could figure out some way to break the bad news. It's too bad Doc Wernitz decided to cash in and pull out all of a sudden like this . . . if you can say cash in."

He listened a moment. "Better give 'em to me, honey. Here comes your mother."

He put them back in the desk drawer and turned the key in the lock. Connie watched him silently. When he turned back she said, "Who else knows about this, Dad?"

"That Janey plays? Why, everybody in town, I expect, honey. Except Gus."

"No, no. I mean about those checks.—Who'd dare tell Gus, I mean."

Her father shrugged. "Doc Wernitz, of course. Then there's Nate Rogers. Jim Ferguson asked him to stop with me, after the Board meeting. His boy Orvie's always been so nice to Janey, maybe Fergie figured he'd help out, if Gus Blake happens to need a quick loan or something. Or maybe Nate Rogers would pass the word to Orvie and Orvie could say something to Janey. They all like Janey, and anyway it's the sort of thing a bank president in a town like this don't want any hard feelin's about."

"*Orvie,*" said Connie Maynard. "It's too bad she didn't marry Orvie and be done with it. He's the one that picked her up and stuck her down everybody's throat. Her father was a night watchman over at the plant and her mother took in roomers. If it hadn't been for Orvie's father's dough she'd still be on Main Street selling peanuts in the dime store."

"Just dry up, honey." His voice was still soft, unchanged, but Connie Maynard knew he meant it. "If it hadn't been for your great-grand-daddy's dough, I'd still be back in the Kentucky mountains, jumpin' gullies to keep ahead of the revenooers."

"Not you, Daddy."

"Maybe not Janey, either, honey.—Here comes your mother."

Connie tilted her elegant tawny head, listening. "No. She's stopped to check the bathrooms—see if the towels are right. You know Mother." She took hold of her father's arm. "Look, Dad. Tell Mr. Rogers and Fergie it's all settled, will you? Tell them you'll talk to Janey. Because listen: Aunt Mamie was in the office again today. She's starting one of her crusades. It's slot machines, this time. She's been driving Gus nearly nuts. He's going to fox her. He's coming out with a blast tomorrow, or next day . . . pro-slot machines, not anti. And if I stop him from . . . you know, making an ass of himself——"

"Why stop him, honey?" John Maynard asked.

She looked at him blankly, her red lips parted. "Why, Dad! No man wants to look like a damn fool——"

"That's what I mean, honey. No man wants to look like a damn fool, but if he makes one of himself he's got to put up with it. What he don't want and can't stand and *don't* have to put up with is his wife makin' a fool out of him."

Connie Maynard dropped his arm and looked straight ahead of her for a moment. "Oh," she said softly. "I see. Now I see."

"Anyway, it's no business of yours to go interferin' in the editorial policy of Gus's newspaper," John Maynard said. "I promised Gus that when he took you on." He smiled at her, listening to his wife's light tread as she crossed the hall toward the library door. He drew Connie's arm into his and patted it affectionately.

A question tinged with something very like despair seemed to flicker through the gray eyes of the frail woman standing in the doorway as she saw the two of them together there.

"Lucy," John Maynard said, "I've been tellin' Connie she's to keep her mouth out of Gus's editorials. If she starts tryin' to dictate to him what he's going to write or not write, I think he ought to fire her."

Lucy Maynard looked at her husband. "I think perhaps he ought to fire her anyway, John.—That's a stunning dress, Connie. Superb theater. Sometime we must have caviare and pressed duck to match it. Everything else is ready, John." She turned her head, listening to the first car coming into the drive. "Please try to keep your sister Mamie from making a speech, John. I'll keep her up here out of the play room if you'll just keep her from drinking too much. I don't know how she became convinced champagne is non-alcoholic. Mamie's temperance lecture when she's hiccoughing never seems the least amusing to me."

TWO

AS THE PARTY was still just beginning, Connie Maynard, balanced on the arm of one of the deep yellow leather sofas that flanked the log-burning fireplace, could still hear herself think and speak without having to scream to make herself heard. And still watch the stairs, smiling, to see Gus and Janey when they came. The cellar of the old house, converted into a play room, was bigger than the Parish Hall and much more comfortable. The sofas in the recesses formed by the arched brick foundations were secluded and cozy, the juke box was still playing sweet and low over in the corner where the bar and games were. The room was slowly filling up now as the crowd divided itself into the older sheep staying soberly upstairs with her father and mother and the younger goats skipping about, down where the fun and noise were.

Connie saw that Orval Rogers was one of them. Not that Orval ever skipped, singly or in pairs. Coming down alone now, his black tie neatly tied, his blond hair neatly brushed, he looked very like a young but sober owl behind his neat steel-rimmed glasses. Halfway down the stairs he stopped, searching the room earnestly for a moment before he came on.

"Poor Orvie . . ."

Connie started a little and looked around. It was Martha Ferguson, wife of the bank president.

"Oh, Martha. You took the words right out of my mind, dear."

It was not quite true, because in her mind they had none of the affectionate warmth and bubbling amusement they had as Martha Ferguson spoke them.

"Hi, Orvie," she said.

"Hi, Connie. Hi, Martha. Dad couldn't come, Connie. He says he's sorry, but he's too old for these routs."

He looked around earnestly again.

"Janey isn't here yet," Connie said.

"Yeah. She said she didn't know whether she could get a sitter for little Jane."

Orvie Rogers wandered over toward the bar. Connie looked around at Martha Ferguson again. "I wonder why we always say 'Poor Orvie,'" she said abruptly. "He's got an awful lot more dough than any of the rest of us."

Martha Ferguson laughed. "Oh, he's so serious and his father makes him work so hard. Poor Orvie—I don't think he's really ever had any fun, or busted out all over. I'm devoted to him. He's really sweet." She took a Manhattan off the tray the colored boy held in front of her. "Now, what I wonder—I mean if we *are* wondering—is how long, for heaven's sakes, we're going on always telling Orvie that Janey hasn't come yet, or

Janey's over there, or Janey's upstairs or out in the garden. It's funny, isn't it?"

"Is it?"

Connie took a sip of the cocktail in her hand. Martha Ferguson glanced at her, her brown eyes kindling a little. "Oh, Connie, don't be a stinker and a louse! You know damn well you've no right to be."

"Darling! Who's being a stinker and a louse? You asked me a question and I asked you another."

"Okay." Martha Ferguson tossed off the rest of her cocktail and put the glass down. "It's not manners to quarrel with your hostess, so I guess I'll move along. I'm a bit tense tonight myself. I *like* Janey."

She let her eyes rest on Connie's plunging neckline and bare smooth shoulders for an instant. "That's a divine little twelve-ninety-eight job you've got on, Connie. Nice for a working girl, I mean. I hope Janey can't find a sitter, if you don't mind my saying so. Though I don't suppose that would keep Gus home." She glanced across the room. "There's my husband wasting his dough on Aunt Mamie's slot machine. I'd better grab him quick, before the rumor starts it's the bank's money he's stuffing down the iron maw."

As she moved away, Connie was alone for a moment in a dancing pool of firelight, her hand resting idly on the back of the yellow sofa, a witch woman smiling quietly as she watched Martha take her husband's arm to pull him away from the slot machine. She watched her cousin Dorsey Syms move in, drop one quarter, shrug and move away for somebody else. If you play the slot machine, that's the way to do it, Connie thought. Take a chance—what was it? 2400 to one on the jackpot, somebody had told her—and not take the second chance that was still 2400 to one. She glanced up the stairs. She could hear her Aunt Mamie's vigorous strident voice and see her in her mind's eye, a champagne glass in one hand, the other firmly pinioning some polite unfortunate, the Rector probably, or the Judge, vocally bludgeoning him on the decay of manners and morals in Smithville, while her son and her husband put their quarters in the machine. Aunt Mamie's slot machine, Martha Ferguson had called it. That was because of the printed sign over it. "This Machine Is For Your Amusement.—It pays off 75 per cent to you and 25 per cent to the box in the corner for the League for Civic Improvement. It does not pay for the liquor you drink here. That's free." It was signed with John Maynard's vigorous scrawl.

Connie turned, smiling, to look up the stairs. The League for Civic

Improvement was the banner under which John Maynard's sister Mamie, otherwise Mrs. Nelson Syms, its founder and president, carried on all her whirlwind crusades. Connie could hear her voice now, rising above the clang of the machines—which must be paying off very well tonight, she thought, the way everybody was crowding in to play it, and judging by the crescendo of the laughing chatter around it.

". . . clubs can't exist in this town without slot machines," Aunt Mamie was saying, "then the clubs will have to fold, my dear Commodore. Bingo is an entirely different matter. The League made twelve hundred dollars on Bingo last year. I myself won an electric mixer, and a very respectable woman I know won a washing machine she very badly needed. That is hardly what I call gambling, Commodore."

"Poor Commodore," Connie thought. She could see him too in her mind's eye, a pleasant little man who was certainly no match for Mrs. Nelson Syms. But the Commodore and Aunt Mamie, Aunt Mamie's son Dorsey Syms whom she'd just seen at the slot machine, Aunt Mamie's husband—Uncle Nelly, he was usually called—and her father's slot machine itself, the gift of Doc Wernitz, there for Amusement and Civic Improvement, occupied only the periphery of Connie Maynard's active mind and smiling attentive eye. Janey and Gus Blake occupied the center and core of both as she watched the stairs, waiting for them to come.

And if they didn't . . . ? If Gus hadn't heard about the checks, he'd certainly come. If he had heard, then he'd have to come, and make her come, just to show, to keep face in front of all their friends. Unless . . . Connie dismissed that. If Janey had been going on month after month, getting deeper and deeper into the hole she'd dug, she wasn't likely to choose tonight to try to crawl out of it, not with Gus so busy trying to get out a Centennial edition of the *Smithville Gazette* that he was hardly civil to his own staff—Gus who by nature and circumstances was never more than six jumps from the sheriff anyway. She could dismiss that. Janey wouldn't tell him tonight even if Janey knew it herself, and nobody else would. Martha Ferguson, maybe—if her husband had told her. Martha might blurt it out for his own good.

Connie looked across the room. The Fergusons were standing at the bar talking to the colored boy behind it, Jim Ferguson's arm around his wife's shoulders. Connie shook her head. Martha talked a lot, but not when Jim told her to shut up. As president of the town's leading bank, this was one time he'd be sure to tell her. No, Gus could go on a long time without knowing anything about it. It was one of the things about a town like Smithville. The Conspiracy of Silence, John Maynard called it. Like Aunt Mamie not knowing she used money from a slot machine, and the people who came and lived there for years not knowing that Judge Dikes hovered so solicitously around his sister because she'd pick up any small movable object if he didn't, and not knowing, for instance, that another of the guests upstairs had shot his wife and been acquitted without the jury's so much as leaving the box to make up their mind.

"Waiting for somebody?"

Connie started. She hadn't noticed her cousin Dorsey Syms move around behind the masonry piers to join her. He was smiling, the Maynard smile. There was very little Syms in Aunt Mamie's son. He had the Maynard height, the Maynard confidence, the black hair, brown eyes, straight nose and slightly cleft chin. And a good deal of his Uncle John Maynard's charm. The Syms family had nothing much to distinguish them except an ancestor who'd conducted the Siege of Smithville against Cornwallis and whom Aunt Mamie had brevetted from ensign to colonel. Except Nelson Syms, of course. He had Aunt Mamie, and the job her brother John Maynard had got him in the County Treasurer's office. And his son Dorsey Syms, whose most attractive quality was his obvious fondness for his father. Neither of them could have survived Aunt Mamie if they hadn't formed a "League" of their own, Connie thought, hearing the voluble determined voice beating on upstairs.

She smiled at her cousin. "Just wondering whether we ought to start feeding people."

"Not before Gus and Janey get here, surely," Dorsey Syms said. "I suppose they're coming?"

"I suppose so."

Not a ripple showed on the clear surface of her casual unconcern, but her pulse had quickened. *He works in the bank. He knows. He must know all about it. He's trying to find out if I know too. He's supposed to have been crazy about Janey once.* She glanced around the play room again. How many people there did know? Jim Ferguson certainly, and probably Martha. Orvie Rogers probably. Dorsey Syms, herself, her father upstairs . . . who else? There were at least thirty people there by now. If Janey and Gus didn't come pretty soon, somebody would say something. . . .

"I hear Doc Wernitz is leaving town," Dorsey said. "Scotch, please." He took a highball off the tray the boy was passing again "Does he take that little gadget of yours over there along with him?"

"You mean the slot machine?"

She wasn't smiling any longer. "That's Dad's, not mine." Her level gaze met his and held it. "And it was a gift, not a loan. Doc Wernitz hasn't any strings on Dad, or vice versa, if that's what you mean. Any more than he has on——"

She broke off and flashed around. The quick light in her cousin's eye and the delighted shout from everybody else in the play room could only mean one of two things. A jackpot, or . . .

"Janey! Hi, Janey!"

A jackpot, Connie Maynard thought, or Janey.

"Hi, Janey!" Everybody was shouting it, and Janey was there on the stairs. Gus was behind her, and Connie heard somebody say, "Hello there, Gus, how's the boy?" But it was Janey they were glad to see and always saw first . . . Janey who always just stopped and stood there, looking as if she'd just been scrubbed and had her hair ribbons tied, always surprised and eternally delighted that they noticed she'd come and really seemed to want her there. Connie Maynard suppressed a sharp flash of irritation. That was what she was doing now, just stopped halfway down the stairs, her small pointed face breaking into wreaths of happiness and delight, her blue eyes like breathless stars, just standing there surprised and excited as a child.—And not even pretty. That irritated Connie Maynard. Her nose was too stubby and turned-up, her face too pointed, her eyes too big and set too far apart, all her facial bones showing, her fuzzy tow-colored hair escaping everywhere as the water she'd slicked it up with dried and it popped out of the black velvet ribbon she wore like a topknot on her head. Janey trying to look sleek and well-groomed was as absurd as her just standing there in the middle of the stairs.

"Go on, Janey." Connie heard Gus Blake, and saw him give her a little push to bring her to.

"Hello, hello, everybody!" She came on down the stairs. "Hello, Connie! I'm sorry we're late." She put her hand out. It was cold, so cold Connie Maynard was startled touching it.

"Hello, Dorsey—hello, Martha!" Janey moved on. "Hello, Orvie— hello, Jim!" Janey never said, "Hi, there" to people. Her voice was always warm and full of velvet delight, as if Connie, Dorsey Syms, Orvie Rogers, Martha and Jim Ferguson, each one of them, was the one person she'd hope could be there without really daring to hope she could count o.. .. and the last person, Connie Maynard thought, in that room,

or in the whole of Smith County, that anybody would think, to look at
her, was responsible for the handsome sheaf of rubber checks upstairs
in John Maynard's library desk drawer. If it made any difference to
anybody what Janey did, it hardly seemed likely, now, the way the
Fergusons, Orvie, Dorsey Syms and all the rest of them gathered
around her.

"Hi there, Gus," Connie said. Gus Blake was left back with her. They
were a little like something washed up on the beach as Janey's trim and
sunlit craft took off to sea. Connie shook her head impatiently. It
wasn't so at all. She could be at the other side of the room with all the
rest of them too, if she wanted to. She was here in the comparative quiet
with Gus because that was the way she wanted it and had maneuvered
to arrange it. *I almost sound as if I'm jealous of Janey.* It came sharply
into her mind. But that was ridiculous. She wasn't in the least jealous of
Janey Blake, only irritated at the way everybody always acted as if
Janey was somehow something different, not just a little climber whose
father was a night watchman at the Rogers plant but something rare and
precious, like a branch of apple blossoms in the snow. How in heaven's
name had Gus Blake ever married her! She felt a sudden passionate
impulse to scream it at him, scream it out at the top of her voice.

She clutched one fist in the green taffeta folds of her skirt.

"Stop it, Connie, stop it!" she told herself angrily. "Just stop it. Don't
·be a fool. Remember you're the girl that has brains."

She forced herself to smile as she looked up at Janey's husband.

"How's the boss man tonight?"

"Pooped," Gus Blake said briefly. "Here comes a drink, and boy,
can I use one. I'd like to throttle whoever it was got the big idea for a
Centennial edition. Thanks, Lawrence, and how about you, Connie?"

Before she could remind him the Centennial edition was his own idea,
originally designed to keep her busy, or even say she didn't want another
drink, Jim Ferguson had disengaged himself from Janey's entourage and
was over with them.

"Hi there, Gus! How's the boy?" He gave Gus an enthusiastic slap on
the back and pumped his hand. "Swell seeing you, boy. Swell party,
Connie. Here comes chow. Well, be seein' you, boy."

He headed off for a table, calling Janey and Orvie Rogers to share it
with him. Gus Blake looked at Connie, one brow quizzically raised.

"What's the matter with our banker?" he inquired. "Vine leaves? Or
is my account overdrawn? Last time Fergie was that glad to see me was

just after he turned me down on some dough I wanted to borrow from his blasted bank."

Connie held her breath for only an instant. There was no meaning in what he'd said. No meaning that he was aware of . . . yet.

"Vine leaves, I expect. Or isn't it barley they make scotch out of? Here's food. Why don't we go back here and sit in peace, if you're pooped."

She moved around to a small table set for two just outside the dancing fan of firelight. Janey was across the room, but Connie could see the blank blue eyes following her and Gus as they got around there, away from the yellow sofas that were filling up with people bringing their plates to eat by the fire. *Janey's the one who's jealous, not me.* It flashed into her mind. Her pulse quickened. Jealousy was stupid. Jealous people did stupid things. And why should Janey care anyway? She had Orvie, Jim Ferguson and Dorsey Syms at her table.

Connie saw suddenly to her irritation that she herself had her uncle Nelson Syms. Uncle Nelly was drawing up a chair to talk to Gus.

"I expect you two see plenty of each other at the paper all day, and I want to ask Gus about that piece Mamie wants to write for the Centennial edition. Her brother said it sure ought to go on the front page, but Mamie'd have to ask you, Gus. John always says he doesn't have any say about the paper; you run it. It's up to you."

Connie bit her lip in sharp vexation. There was nothing she could do. Poor Uncle Nelly. Thin and stoop-shouldered, he looked as if he'd been brought up in a potato cellar before a steam roller had permanently shaped him. Sometimes she wondered what would have happened to Uncle Nelly if Aunt Mamie hadn't married him and forced him to live their kind of life, moving him from job to job until John Maynard got him the one he'd had for ten years now, as a clerk in the County Treasurer's office. He'd probably have been a lot happier and never had the stomach ulcers that put him in the hospital a couple of weeks out of every year.

He was going on about Aunt Mamie's article, and Gus Blake was listening, not irritably or even patiently, but with a friendly interest that apparently was quite genuine, sipping his highball, nodding his head, as serious about this nonsense, apparently, as Uncle Nelly himself. Anybody would think Uncle Nelly was one of his closest friends and most astute advisers, the way he was listening . . . or think he was glad to have Uncle Nelly there so he wouldn't be alone in the corner with her. But that was nonsense too.

"I wonder if I'll ever really understand the guy," Connie Maynard thought, trying to blot out her uncle's voice. It had the unbearable monotony of a tap dripping in a basement laundry tub. She lowered her eyes and looked through her long darkened lashes at the man across the table from her, the editor of her father's paper, her boss whose job she could take any time she decided she really wanted it . . . even if she and everybody else knew she couldn't do it as well as he did. He had a flair for it that she didn't have, even if he didn't have courage enough to say nuts to the local customers and take their obituaries off the front page and put them over on page ten where they belonged. That was the first thing she'd do. And she'd get along. She'd keep Ed Noonan as city editor, just as Gus had done. She brought herself up sharply. That wasn't what she wanted. She didn't want the paper. She wanted Gus Blake and the paper. The paper was hers any time she wanted it. Her father could give it to her with sound financial logic, saving on his income tax now and estate taxes later, since the *Gazette,* tottering on its last moribund typestick when Gus took it over, had showed a very neat profit for three years running. But it wasn't the paper. It was Gus Blake.

"Because I'm absolutely nuts about this guy," Connie Maynard thought.

THREE

HER PULSE QUICKENED again as she glanced across the table at him. The sound of his voice, the half-sardonic twist of his wide mouth when he smiled, the sudden subrisive humor that lighted his gray eyes without apparent reason a hundred times a day . . . all of it added up to something that set up jet pinpoints of flame inside her far more exciting than anything else she'd ever known. And infinitely more exciting now she was back home after her own trial fling at marriage, with Janey a barrier between them, than he'd ever been when she was engaged to him, and could have had him simply by being a little less willful and impatient.

"I was a fool," she thought. "No. I wasn't. This is a lot more fun. There were things I had to learn."

As she looked at him again, pushing his plate away and getting a cigarette out of his pocket, squinting as he took the candle from the middle of the table to light it, Connie smiled to herself.

"Maybe it's just the old Œdipus complex after all. I could get it psyched out of me and save a lot of trouble."

He was very like her father, except that his hair was a crisp sandy ginger instead of iron-gray. He was as tall and strongly built, his shoulders had the same slight stoop, he moved in the same relaxed and easy-going fashion and with the same deceptive calm, concealing both power and energy, different in kind and perhaps used for different purposes, but the same in quality and latent reserve. Nobody would ever shove either of them twice. She knew that about her father. Jim Ferguson had proved it about Gus by passing the buck to her father in the form of Janey's checks. Other people would get a routine notice in the morning mail. Or Doc Wernitz would have got the checks bounced back to him, like a lot of others he'd got back from Smithville's slot machine addicts, written in their avid search for fool's gold. Fergie had done neither to Gus, whose bank balance was always precariously low and a matter of apparent indifference to him. And there was something odd somewhere . . . something odd about all of it that she couldn't quite put her finger on at the moment.

She shrugged it off. Gus's bank balance wasn't precariously low now. It was non-existent, with three hundred and twenty strikes on it in the form of Janey's checks in her father's drawer. And it was her father's fault, in a way. She knew Gus was paid about half what he was worth, in terms of what he had made the paper pay or what her father would have had to pay anybody else as good, or not as good. There must have been some sort of a deal. She suspected that without knowing it, but she knew one thing for sure: Gus, not her father, would be the one gypped in the end. That was one thing about John Maynard's deals. Like the slot machine over there in the corner. If the twenty-five per cent—and it was a lot nearer forty—that went to the League for Civic Improvement hadn't come out of their friends' pockets, John Maynard would have had to put it up out of his own, just to keep Aunt Mamie out of his hair. It was all good clean fun, and it was still a gyp.

Connie pushed her chair back and looked over at the corner. The machine was rattling away again now that people were through supper.

Janey was still at the table with Orvie Rogers and Jim Ferguson. Martha Ferguson was at the slot machine with Dorsey Syms, Martha putting in the quarters and Dorsey pulling down the iron arm. It came down then, with the tinkle of a coin and an empty metallic sound, and suddenly both Martha and Dorsey Syms thrust their arms out around it.

"Hey, Janey! Come on, Janey!" Both of them were calling her. "Come on, Janey! We know this machine—it's ready to give! Come on, Janey!"

Connie Maynard had never heard Martha Ferguson so excited before. Her cheeks tingled. "My God," she thought, "they'll even stand aside for her to take their dough in a thirty-dollar jackpot!" She was aware that she had got up abruptly and was standing gripping the back of her chair, watching everybody crowd forward, everybody shouting, "Come on, Janey, it's your turn at the jackpot!" Everybody but Gus Blake. She looked around at him. He was still lounging lazily there on the seat in the corner behind the table, his wide mouth twisted in his semi-sardonic smile, relaxed and waiting for the tumult to die down.

"Come on, Janey!"

Janey had not moved. She was sitting bolt upright at her table, shaking her head, shaking out what was left of the mop of tow-colored fuzz tied with the velvet bow.

"No," she said. She shook her head again. "I'm not going to play."

"Oh, come on, Janey. Come on, be a sport. Just two quarters, Janey. Look, nobody's won it for three weeks."

Jim Ferguson was pointing up to the framed cardboard bulletin behind the bar. "Look, Janey, the last jackpot was in October. Nelly won it in October."

Connie glanced at the board. It was a record of the jackpots, the dates and winners—all part of the fine high plausibility that made Doc Wernitz's Christmas gift to her father all open and above-board and for Amusement Only. *And keeps our play room different from an ordinary clip joint* . . . She turned sharply and looked at Gus Blake, her cheeks flushing. She'd said it to herself, but it was what he was thinking too. She could tell by the amused glint in his eyes before his craggy face broke into an open grin.

"Relax, Con," he said. "Or is it against the house rules for the customers to get a break?" He looked over at his wife. "Go on, Janey. We can use thirty bucks—if you get it."

For a fraction of an instant Connie Maynard felt really sorry for the

girl. "She's scared. She's terribly scared," she thought. "And she ought
to be. Even I'd be scared, in her shoes."

She turned her head. One of the colored boys had come down the
steps and was beckoning to Gus.

"Telephone, Mr. Blake." He motioned to the recess behind the stairs.
"It's the paper."

Connie felt her cheeks flush again as Gus got instantly to his feet.
Now it was the paper. First it was her Uncle Nelly, then all the jackpot
and Janey business, absorbing his attention in spite of all her maneuver-
ing. Now the paper. The paper was the only thing he really gave a damn
about, she thought irritably, glancing resentfully at his broad back as he
reached the stairs, everybody still clamoring for Janey to come and win
the jackpot.

"Go on, Janey, and maybe they'll all shut up." He stopped at the
foot of the stairs and grinned at his wife before he went on around to
answer the phone.

Janey's lips moved in a wooden smile. She pushed her chair back
from the table. With the stiff movement of her young body the black
velvet bow came loose and toppled into her lap. She picked it up, untied
the bow, caught her hair and pulled it up, tying it into a topknot again.
Then she raised her pointed little face. It was pinched and pale and her
eyes were like black smudges. She tried to smile as she got to her feet.

"You're all . . . you're all terribly sweet. I . . . I'd love to get a
jackpot, but I . . . I never do."

She moved with the curious grace of a wooden doll across to the
machine, fishing in her bag.

Orvie Rogers sprang forward. "Here, Janey, I'll lend you some
quarters."

"No, thanks. I've got one. Maybe two—I don't know." She took
another step forward to the machine.

"Come on, Janey. Don't let Dorsey pull it for you. He'll jinx it,
Janey!"

Somebody shouted that, but it sounded disproportionately loud and
raucous. Everybody else was suddenly tense and silent. It was like that
moment at the race track when a hundred people hold their breath as
the hundred-to-one shot pulls ahead of the favorite at the finish. It was
absurd. Connie Maynard felt that sharp chill prickle across her bare
shoulders and down her spine. Janey raised her hand, hesitating an instant before she put the coin in the slot. She reached over quickly, took

hold of the iron handle, pulled it down and dropped it as if it had
burned into her hand. The reels spun through the harshly colored,
blurred cycle of cherries, lemons, oranges, plums and bells, spun the
full cycle and whirred in turn to a stop: a cherry, another cherry, and
an orange. Then came the final click, sharp and still curiously hollow,
and the jingle of the three quarters falling.

"Leave 'em in, Janey—leave 'em in for a nest egg!" some one
shouted. "One more, Janey!"

"Go on, Janey. One more. I know this machine." It was Martha
Ferguson who said that. She spoke quietly, but it sounded oddly like
a command, as if thirty people there each willing the machine to pay
must in some way make it pay. Janey Blake stood there motionless for
a moment, her slight body rigid in front of the garishly painted machine,
tensed sharply. She straightened her shoulders. Her tow head went up
in a small gesture of defiance.—Defiance, or was it pride? Connie Maynard, unconsciously gripping the back of her chair again, her own body
as rigid as Janey's, saw it as Janey's hand went quickly out. She dropped
the quarter, yanked down the arm and flashed around.

"There," she said. "That's that." She took three steps forward, her
eyes swimming blindly, her face white, her chin up. She took another
step toward her table and had put her hand out to reach for it when the
room broke into delighted tumultuous cheers.

"Jackpot! Janey! Janey! It's a jackpot, Janey!"

Some of the quarters burst out over the cup, metal ringing on the
tiled floor as everybody scrambled, laughing and excited, to pick up
Janey's jackpot out of the corners. One came rolling across the room,
spinning crazily at least an inch from Connie Maynard's green slip-
per. She put her foot out and stopped it without moving her eyes from
Janey's rigid figure by the table. Her hand was still out. She was bal-
ancing herself against the table, her face blank and white, blind and
deaf.

"Deaf, blind and very dumb," Connie Maynard thought sharply.
She didn't seem to realize she'd won the jackpot, or that it might have
been for a thousand dollars the way Smithville's elite were laughing and
scrambling around on all fours picking up her rolling take. Jim Ferguson, president of the leading bank, and Martha his wife. Orvie Rogers, son of the richest man in the county. Doctor, lawyer, merchant,
chief. To say nothing of Dorsey Syms, rising young banker, and his

father Uncle Nelly. Or herself for that matter, she thought, bending down and picking up the quarter at her feet.

"Here," she said. She thrust it into Jim Ferguson's hand. "Give her this one too."

He looked down at it, the banker's caution so automatic that she laughed for the first time since Janey and Gus had come. "It rolled out, Jim. Right over at my feet. If it's a counterfeit, some kind friend put it in."

He was already bursting back across the room to Janey.

"Look, Janey! Here's a gold quarter, somebody's lucky piece! It's a quarter with gold wash—it's your lucky piece, Janey!" He opened her evening bag and thrust it inside, and dumped the rest of the quarters he'd picked up onto the pile on the table. "Come on, everybody. Bring out your folding money."

"—What's all this? What's all this noise and racket?" Connie looked quickly over at the stairs. The screaming and laughter had brought her father down. John Maynard was bending over the banisters, handsome and smiling, as happy as everybody else. "What's going on down here?"

"It's Janey, John." Jim Ferguson pointed to the shining pile of coins heaped on the table. "Janey won the jackpot."

"Oh, good for Janey!"

If he had won it himself John Maynard could not have been more pleased. He reached in his pocket for his billfold. "How much, Jim?"

The president of the bank finished counting. "Thirty-two fifty, unless somebody's holding out on us."

"Fine." John Maynard took the bills out of his wallet. He looked across the room. "Phone Doc Wernitz, will you, Connie? Tell him the jackpot's hit and to come over and set the machine up again. Maybe Janey'll get another. Here, Jim, give Janey this. Janey, there ain't nobody, honey, I'd rather——"

With the gold-washed lucky piece and counting Janey's quarters to put them into portable form, everybody had forgotten Janey for a moment, and everybody but Constance Maynard had forgotten Gus. He had come out of the cubicle behind the stairs and had stopped, his gray eyes hard as stone, looking over at Janey, as everybody else was looking at her then. She was standing there, not wooden any more or rigid, but trembling, shaking from the black velvet bow on the top of her head to the soles of her gold-slippered feet. The tears were streaming down her cheeks.

"Janey!" Orvie Rogers sprang forward. "Janey! What's the———"

"No, no—don't! Let me alone! Let me alone!"

She broke loose from Orvie Rogers and Martha Ferguson and ran blindly, choking back her sobs, through the mute and staggered crowd, past her husband and past John Maynard up the stairs, tripping at the top but catching herself and on out of sight.

Gus Blake took a step toward her and stopped again, a light in his eyes that was new to Connie Maynard, new and almost unbearably exciting, neither amused nor sardonic and least of all lazy or detached.

He said quietly, "Maybe somebody here better tell me what in hell's the matter with my child bride. Or maybe I'd better tell you something."

He turned and looked up the stairs. "There's no use Connie's calling Doc Wernitz to reset the machine, Maynard. Doc Wernitz is dead. They've just found him down in his cellar, his skull smashed with an iron bar. Somebody murdered Doc Wernitz a couple of hours ago— while everybody here was having a quick drink and getting into his black tie, white shirt and dinner coat."

He turned back to Connie Maynard. "Go up and get Janey, will you? I'll take her home first."

"Orvie can take Janey home."

Who it was said that, in the intense silence of the room, Connie Maynard did not know.

"I'll take her home," Gus Blake said shortly.

He knows about Janey. As Connie Maynard thought it, a sharp quiver of excitement ran through her. There was something in the way he said it. . . . She caught herself up quickly. Or was it something else? What could there be about the killing of the little gambler none of them could have known that had created instantly the extraordinary tension she could feel now in the room? It was so real and electric that she could feel it to the tips of her fingers as she slipped across to the stairs and up to go after Janey. She could feel it implicit in Gus Blake's voice as she heard him again and stopped at the head of the stairs to listen.

"I didn't know Doc Wernitz myself, but I knew something about him. He was a pretty decent sort of guy, for the racket he was in. I don't like the idea of his being murdered. So don't anybody here call up the *Gazette* tomorrow and try to tell me to lay off, and that Smithville doesn't want to get mixed up with gamblers getting what's coming to them. You're all gamblers, friends, and tomorrow I'm telling you all why I think it's okay for suckers to play Doc's slot machines."

He started up the stairs and stopped. "And don't get me wrong, pals," he said evenly. "I'm not condoning you, or the machines. Personally and privately, I think you both stink. So if you'll excuse me now, I'll go out and see what happened."

FOUR

GUS BLAKE brought the car to a lurching stop and reached over across Janey to open the door. Maybe he should have left her at the Maynards' and let Orvie Rogers bring her home later, but their house was on the way to Doc Wernitz's at Newton's Corner, and home in bed was obviously where she belonged. He tried to make her face out in the light coming through the dusty windshield from the overhead traffic signal on the corner. All he could see was a greenish seasick blob above the black velvet collar of her evening wrap.

"You sure you'll be okay, Janey? I've got to get out there before they start pushing things around. There's something screwy about this. You can smell it a mile."

"I'm okay, Gus."

"You don't sound it."

As the light changed, turning the greenish cast of her face into a rosy red, she looked a little better anyway. She pulled herself forward in the seat.

"I'm all right, Gus. You go ahead. I *told* you I'm all right now."

"Sure, you told me. I still don't get it. I don't see anything about getting a thirty-two-fifty jackpot that's enough to make you blow your top the way you did. But there's no use our yakking about it any more. You're a wreck." He opened the door. "You go on in and go to bed. Get your mother to stay all night. I'll make up the couch if I get home in time to need it. Okay?"

"Okay." Janey pulled her skirt around her legs and got out, holding on to the door to steady her wooden knees. She took a step and turned back.

"—What is it, Janey?"

He didn't mean to sound abrupt or impatient, but he was in a hurry. When he'd said there was something screwy about Wernitz's murder he meant it. Smithville was not in any of the big-time gambling circuits. As such things went, Doc Wernitz had operated quietly and reasonably within the law. But slot machines and murder had teamed up before. If Doc Wernitz had been killed earlier, it might easily have been written off as an occupational hazard. Coming now, just as the news that he was shutting up shop and leaving Smithville had barely begun to trickle out into the open, it was something else again.

And what had the great Blake done when the counter man at the Margot Lunch had told him, that evening at six o'clock, that he'd heard Doc Wernitz was leaving? Blake, the Narcissus, had looked at himself in the black pool of the Margot's lousy coffee and wondered whether he ought to go back and pull his trenchant and thought-provoking editorial reply to Aunt Mamie on the slot machines, and decided against it. There'd always be another Wernitz to operate the machines, and always suckers to play them. That, plus a commendable caution on his part: he didn't want anybody in Smithville saying he'd written the editorial and then hot-footed it out to Wernitz for his approval—which is what they'd say if he'd been seen within a mile of Newton's Corner that or any other day.

And now it was too late. At that moment, or a little earlier, or a little later, Doc Wernitz had been murdered. He gave himself a vicious kick in the seat of his mental pants, setting up a chain reaction that made his voice sound sharper and more impatient as he repeated his question. "What is it now? I'm in one hell of a hurry."

"I'm sorry."

She drew back quietly. The light in the corner behind them switched to red, but the convertible coming along the street speeded up and shot through, live rubber screaming on the pavement as it slid to a sharp stop behind Gus Blake's dingy coupé. Janey stiffened. It was too late for her to get the door shut. Connie Maynard was already there.

"I'm going with you, Gus. Come on, let me drive you."

She was at the car door, holding it open, bending forward as she talked to him. Janey moved back. They hadn't pushed her away, not physically, but the effect was the same. Her long black velvet skirt brushed the dry leaves in front of the hedge, her high heels tottered on the uneven bricks. Connie had low-heeled shoes on and a tweed coat lined with fur.

"You go back home, Connie."

Janey heard him, but she heard Connie too.

"I'm going with you," she said coolly. She laughed. "A reporter's place is at her editor's side. I've never been in on a murder, Gus, and it's good experience, and I'm going, whether you like it or not. I've got a press card too. You'd better let me drive you. I can make better time than you can and not have a flat half way there."

She pulled the door back with a determined hand. "Come on, Gus. Don't be a stubborn ape. We've got to hurry."

Janey put her key into the lock and held on to the doorknob for a moment, her eyes closed, trying to swallow down the hollow sick waves of despair coming up from inside her stomach. Gus was gone, in Connie's car. It was her own fault. He'd much rather drive himself than have even Connie drive him, but what she'd said about a flat was true. He had to drive at a snail's pace on the graveled corduroy roads out in the country. They could have had new tires—they could have had a new car—if it hadn't been for her.

She let her burning forehead rest on the cold white surface of the door. How much was it? A thousand dollars? It couldn't be. There wasn't that much money in the whole world. It couldn't be a thousand dollars. That was crazy. She couldn't possibly have written that many checks, for ten dollars, or twenty dollars. There had to be something wrong somewhere. She raised her head, shook it violently to shake off the sick, horrible web of fear weaving itself around her mind, and turned the key in the lock. It was true, of course. There was no use denying it, no use lying to herself, pretending what was true couldn't be true.

It came again, the horrible sickening moment of torture as the truth flashed nakedly and clearly into her mind, before the intensity of it numbed and paralyzed her so that she could go on living with it inside her until it came again, suddenly like this, or earlier when the jackpot fell there at the Maynards'. She clenched her fists and pressed her head harder against the wood of the door. "Oh, no, no," she whispered. "It can't be." It couldn't be a thousand dollars. It couldn't possibly have added up to that much in the ten- and fifteen- and once in a while twenty-dollar checks she'd written and cashed at the Sailing Club and the Country Club. There had to be something wrong somewhere. The bank balance would have showed it over the last five months. The scribbled check stubs she'd torn out and stuck in her pocket, put away then and only got out and added up the week before, must be wrong. She

must have made duplicates of some of them. That had to be it, or they'd
have been turned in to the bank and showed on her balance. She'd kept
telling herself that, half believing it at first, sharply repressing the whispering doubt telling her it was more likely to be the other way, that
these weren't all, there were others she'd written and forgotten about
and hadn't put down. . . . More than a thousand dollars. . . . It
couldn't be. She'd kept telling herself that, with only a few icy prickles
in her heart to tell her the truth, multiplying every time she added the
check stubs again, until they'd turned suddenly into a freezing, sickening deluge there was no possibility of denying . . . and with it had
come the paralyzing horrible fear weaving its web around her. It was
true, and there was nothing she could do about it. The money was gone,
there was no way to bring it back.

She knew it was true, and she'd even known it would be true, since
she'd first started playing the slot machines in June, the month after
Constance Maynard came back home and started working with Gus on
the paper. She'd known it but she hadn't cared, at first. There was
something about yanking down the iron handle of the machine that
seemed to take the sickening loneliness out of her life. Every time she
yanked at it she was yanking at Constance Maynard; every time she
put in a quarter, or a half dollar, and yanked the iron handle she was
transferring unhappiness, and resentment, and fear, from Gus and the
woman who was the cause of it to the blatant inanimacy of the machine. It didn't matter if she won or lost. At least she wasn't at home,
alone, while Gus and Connie covered the waterfront—the sailing races,
the stock shows, the tobacco auctions, the city council and county commissioners' meetings . . . Gus conducting a private school of jour-
nalism with the owner's daughter as sole pupil.

"Why don't you leave the kid with your mother, Janey, and go down
to the Club with Orvie? Connie and I'll join you for dinner when we
get back. You'd be bored stiff, Janey. It's just a demonstration of contour ploughing." If it wasn't contour ploughing it was something else
she wouldn't be interested in. "—Why don't you go with Orvie on his
boat, Janey? All they do at the finish line is sit around and have another drink, and you don't drink, Janey." And in August they'd decided they'd put out a Centennial edition of the *Smithville Gazette*.
"Where's Orvie, Janey? He'll take you to the dance. We've got to work
tonight."

"—And I'm not married to Orvie—I'm married to Gus!"

It was a hurt, passionate protest that pulled her sharply up, bringing her back face to face with another reality that the jingle, clank and whirr of the slot machines helped her momentarily to forget.

"Oh, I wish I were . . ." She didn't say the rest of it. Some kind of primitive fear that the spoken wish had a magic power of its own stopped her. You had to be sure before you said what you wished, sure it was what you really wanted. . . . But it was what she wanted. Not because of the slot machines and the thousand dollars. If it hadn't been for all the rest of it there'd never have been any slot machines. She'd never played them, or wanted to play them, until everything else went out of her life when Constane Maynard came back into Gus's.

He should never have married me. I should have known I wasn't good enough for him.—A thousand dollars . . . Her mind flashed back to it. Real and tangible as it was, it was more than just a thousand dollars; it was a symbol into which she had translated all her loneliness and despair. *Oh, I wish I were dead* . . .

She had said it. You say things, and it's one step further. She clutched the small black velvet bag tighter in her hand, her lips suddenly dry as ashes. Inside it, there was another step. She closed her eyes tightly for a moment. Then she raised her chin, opened her eyes and took a long breath of the cold November air. Her mother was staying with little Jane. She couldn't let her mother see, and she had a way of seeing when things were wrong.

She opened the door. "Hello, mother. It's me."

She called up the stairs, expecting her mother would be there in the living room, dozing in front of the fire over her knitting. It was a small house in the center of the town, old brick, two rooms deep, three stories high, set back from the street behind a high privet hedge, with a long narrow back yard; the kitchen and dining room on the first floor, the living room and Gus's study on the second and their bedroom in front, little Jane's in back on the third, with a bathroom in between at the head of the narrow crooked staircase up the side of the house. It was a good house if a crazy one, built by a man who wanted to have a small grocery store on the ground floor and rooms to live in above, that Gus had found, and that had become to Janey the core of a vivid rainbow dream . . . a dream that had started changing five months ago, slowly at first, and gathering speed until at last it had broken into a nightmare of despair and disillusion.

"Mother!" she called again. The double doors from the hall into the dining room were open, and the other door leading into the pantry. The light in the kitchen was on. Her mother came bustling happily out, wiping her hands on a yellow-and-white-checked dishtowel.

"I thought I'd just make you children a coffee cake after little Jane went to sleep," she said briskly. "I didn't expect you home this early." She stopped wiping her hands, the smile on her face fading. "Why, Janey, what's the matter?" She put the dishtowel down on the pantry table and came through the dining room. "What is it, Janey?"

For an instant the tenderness and anxiety in her mother's face almost betrayed her. She turned quickly and took off her evening wrap. As she dropped it on the chair she saw her mother's old gray coat on it, neatly folded across the back. Her black cotton gloves and worn black handbag were on the table. A thousand dollars . . . It was almost half of what her father made in a year at the Rogers plant—and with that and what her mother had made sewing and renting the spare room to a foreman in the shipping department they had brought Janey up and owned their own house, and even had a second-hand car now that Janey was married. They'd even saved something for their own kind of social security.

"It's nothing, mother."

Her mother was still standing there looking at her.

"Where's Gus, Janey?"

Janey put her hand on the chair to steady her knees.

"He had to go out in the country." She moistened her lips so she could speak. "Some man was killed. A man named Doc Wernitz——"

"I know," her mother said. "I heard it on the radio." Her voice was brisk and matter-of-fact again. "He was a gambler. He ran all these machines—supposed to give you something for nothing and never do. The Smithville Recreation Company. If that's what they call recreation. Janey!"

Janey was staring at her, her eyes drained of color. *The Smithville Recreation Company.* The words were an inaudible whisper scarcely moving her lips. That was what was stamped in red on the back of many of the ten- and twenty-dollar checks she'd written to the Sailing Club that the bank had returned with her statements the first of the month. "Pay to the Smithville Recreation Company." It was stamped in red letters on the back . . . of a few hundred dollars' worth of all the checks she'd written.

"Janey, what *is* the matter with you?" her mother demanded. "Everybody knew Mr. Wernitz was the Smithville Recreation Company."

Everybody but Janey. It went slowly through her mind. *I didn't know.*

"And now they've murdered him." It was a statement of simple fact, the event neither surprising nor regrettable, the way her mother said it. Then, as if she had not meant it to sound as callous as it did, she said, "But it's a pity all the same. I'm sorry for the poor man. He wasn't a bad sort, just by himself. Dad'll miss him dropping by the plant on hot nights, to visit out on the pier."

Janey swayed dizzily. Her mother's voice seemed a long way off, reaching her through a swarm of angry bees buzzing in red stamped letters around her. It seemed as if her mother was saying her father knew Doc Wernitz, and Doc Wernitz used to visit with him. But it couldn't be. She was too dazed to hear.

"In fact, he was a lonely sort of man, your father always said." Her mother went over to the chair and took her coat. "His people came from the same place in the old country Dad's came from. I guess Dad'll miss him, if nobody else does. I guess your father was the only friend he had. Real friend, I mean."

She put on her coat. Janey stood motionless. The swarming bees had gone away. Everything seemed curiously quiet and very clear. Doc Wernitz was the Smithville Recreation Company. He was the one who cashed checks for the Country Club and the Sailing Club when the banks were closed and they'd run out of silver. He was a friend of her father's. He hadn't banked all of her checks he'd taken. That explained why so few of them showed on her monthly statement from the bank. The cold fear caught again at her heart. What did it mean? Had he just kept them because her father was his friend?

She went uncertainly through the doors into the cool shadows of the dining room and let herself down into a chair, holding tightly to the edge of the table to keep from missing the chair and falling to the floor. Had he told her father? What if some of her checks, the ones he had not taken to the bank, were out at his house? What if Gus found them? What if Connie Maynard, out there now with Gus, found them? As she closed her eyes she could feel herself thinking: *if only I didn't have to open them again, and ever look at any one again* . . .

"Janey." Her mother had started to the front door, but she came back into the dining room. Her shadow in front of the lamp on the hall table threw a merciful darkness across the table where Janey sat.

"Yes, mother."—How could she sit there in the crumbled ruins of her small universe and say, "Yes, mother," as if nothing had happened and nothing mattered?

"I don't know what's the matter, Janey, but I know you don't act like yourself any more, so it must mean you and Gus are having trouble. It's what Dad and I were afraid was going to happen when you were so bent and determined on marrying him. There was nothing anybody could say to you, you were so crazy in love with him. Dad wanted you to marry Orvie Rogers, because Orvie is a good boy, even if he didn't want you at first to run around with Orvie's crowd instead of boys of your own kind and condition. And Dad never thought Gus would marry you, Janey. The way you were, blind and deaf and dumb to everything else, Dad and I were worried sick all the time. You were so crazy mad after him. And if Constance Maynard hadn't gone off and left him the way she did, there's no telling what would have happened. She was the one he was in love with. Everybody in town knew that. He was never any part as crazy about you as you were about him."

"I know it." She tried to speak it, but no sound came. She knew it very well. It was that other reality she faced and tried desperately to forget each time she yanked down the handle of the slot machine. It was the thing she knew each time Gus said, "Why don't you get Orvie to take you?" It was the answer, every time she cried out to herself in protest that it was not Orvie but Gus she was married to.

She moistened her lips again. "I know it, mother. You don't have to remind me."

"Somebody's got to remind you. I'm not doing it just to hurt you. You've got little Jane to think of, Janey. I'm glad to come and sit here when you and Gus want to go out and Dad's at work. I like to do it. But not if it makes you forget Gus has his work and you have yours. And that's most likely what's the matter with you right now, with that Maynard girl working on the paper and all. I guess you're worried, worried sick, Janey. But Gus is your husband. I don't think he's apt to forget as easy as you think. Gus never looked to Dad and me like a man that lets anybody pull him around by the nose."

She patted Janey's shoulder. "What if I worried all my life because there were a lot of pretty girls working the same place Dad worked?

Good night, Janey. You better go and see that little Jane hasn't kicked the covers off. It's cold tonight."

The front door closed behind her. Janey listened to her step on the frosty pavement until it was gone and the house was silent except for the hum of the oil burner in the basement and the icebox motor coming on and going off.

"—You've never thrown away a thousand dollars," she whispered. "You've never wished you could go to bed and go to sleep and never have to wake again . . ."

She pushed her chair back from the table and got to her feet. The black evening bag was on the table in the hall. Her feet were like blocks of frozen wood as she went over to it and picked it up. She held it for a moment and opened it. There were the thirty-two dollars in bills on top, that Constance Maynard had stuffed in there, with her handkerchief, and some quarters that dropped on the table as she took the bills out. One of them was the gilded quarter that Jim Ferguson had put in her bag. Somebody's lucky piece. Her lucky piece, Jim had said. She turned it over in her hand, dropped it back in the bag and put the other quarters with the bills on the table.

The other thing was in the bag too. She shivered as she took it out. It was a piece of yellow cleansing tissue, the corners twisted together to make a small pouch. Her fingers trembled as she untwisted it and held it open in the palm of her hand under the lamp on the table. A dozen small oblong capsules glittered up at her, a dozen small evil orange-colored eyes. ". . . *go to sleep and never have to wake up again* . . ." She stared blindly down at them. Then she raised her head, listening up the stairs, and drew a sudden breath of sharp and passionate decision. She jerked her hand back and flung them violently away from her, knocking her bag after them onto the rug. The evil orange eyes rolled off the rug onto the waxed pine floor and lay winking up at her. The guilded lucky piece flew out of the bag, rolled off in a crazy half-circle and back near her feet. It winked up too. She bent down breathlessly and picked it up. Maybe it really was her lucky piece. She pressed it in her closed palm an instant before she picked up her bag and dropped it in. Then very slowly she gathered up the orange-colored capsules and put them back in the square of tissue. She got to her feet and counted them. There were only eleven. She got down again to look for the twelfth. It must have rolled into the dining room. She turned on the light and looked there, but it was nowhere in sight and she was suddenly too tired to look any more.

In the morning. She folded the eleven up in the tissue and picked up her bag, too tired to find the last one now, too tired even to go out and turn off the kitchen light. She put her foot on the first step, and on the second. A thousand dollars . . . She might as well have flushed it down the bathroom drain, the way she was going to do with the orange-colored capsules. She clutched them a little tighter in her hand. A thousand dollars . . . It couldn't be. It couldn't possibly be.

FIVE

GUS BLAKE shifted his hundred and ninety pounds from his left haunch to his right. He was trying actually to shift his mind so he could concentrate on the garishly lighted room he was now in, to get rid of the image in it, of the basement downstairs and the little man lying in front of the fuse box, the side of his head smashed in, the blood drying on the earth floor, oozing out of his head again as Swede Carlson, Chief of the County Police, turned him over. And his face . . . the black cobwebs plastered to it, covering it like a filthy obscene veil. The fuse box was above him on the grimy whitewashed stone foundation walls. The center fuse that had been taken out was back in again. It had controlled the center lights in this room. Gus squinted up at them now and looked about the room. This was the battered roll-top desk where Wernitz had been sitting. A cigarette just lighted had burned down to an unbroken column of gray ash in the copper tray. An opened fountain pen lay on a paper beside it, the high-backed swivel chair was quarter-turned, facing the hall door. Doc Wernitz had been working there when the three lights in the room went off, leaving the hall light on. He had put down his cigarette and his pen and gone through the hall and down the basement steps with no idea that the momentary easily repaired darkness he'd left would turn in one instant to another irreparable darkness. It was ruthlessly and hideously simple.

Gus shifted his weight again. Beside him, Swede Carlson, his broad posterior propped solidly against the edge of the rolltop desk, listened stolidly as Gus listened with rising irritation to the County Attorney, speaking officially and for publication to the representative of the *Smithville Gazette,* who stood notebook in hand taking it down. The County Attorney was at the far end of the room, in front of the grimy barred window, hammering it just enough to make it look good in the picture the *Gazette* photographer was taking.

"You can say we've got all the angles covered, Miss Maynard. There's never been any organized crime in Smith County, and there's not going to be."

Gus Blake was aware of a rasping in his left ear. It sounded like sandpaper taking rust off an iron grate. He heard it again and assorted it this time into words. "—Get this dame out of here, Blake."

"You can say we're all on the same team, here in Smith County, Miss Maynard. We're putting everything we've got in this. Every law enforcement officer in Smith County has his nose to the grindstone and his shoulder to the wheel."

The County Attorney stopped, waited for the camera flash, and relaxed. He turned to Swede Carlson. "Anything you want to add, Chief?"

"I guess that about covers it, Frank."

Hearing the faintly sardonic inflection, Gus remembered what Swede Carlson had said down in the basement about the Filipino boy Buzz Rodriguez now sitting out in the hall under guard, waiting to be thrown into the Smithville County Jail. The County Attorney's oblique glance across the room included both of them. He turned back to Connie Maynard. "One other thing. I want to make it clear that any rumors suggesting a scapegoat in this affair are false. The people of Smith County will have no doubt where they come from. And you can say Chief Carlson is in charge and giving the case his personal attention."

He picked his hat up off a chair. "I think that's all I can do here tonight. Can I take you back to town, Miss Maynard?"

"No, I've got my car, Mr. Hamilton," Connie Maynard said. She closed her notebook and looked at Gus. "What now?" she was asking.

Swede Carlson's elbow dug into his ribs. It was as eloquent as his low-rasped, "Get that dame out of here."

Connie Maynard was still looking at him. "Go out and have a look at the kitchen and pantry, Con," he said. "Woman's angle. Bachelor Hall stuff."

Her green eyes sharpened.

"Go on," he said coolly. "And when you're through you can run along home. The Chief'll take me in."

For a moment as the suspicion changed to anger in her eyes he thought she was refusing. The County Attorney had his overcoat on and his hat in his hand. "Come on, Miss Maynard. I'll show you the kitchen. I'd like to have another look at it myself. Attention to detail is what counts, in cases like this."

As the door closed a wintry smile passed through Chief Carlson's bleak eyes. He said, "Never liked dames messin' around where they don't belong. Makes me nervous." He moved his heavy nerveless body off the edge of the desk. "Okay, fella. What do *you* know?"

"I came out to ask you."

Gus looked around the room. It extended the length of the house, with two windows at the back and one at each side of the fireplace in the side wall. The back windows were barred with iron grids fixed solidly in the wall. The side windows were blocked, one with a heavy steel filing cabinet, the other with an old-fashioned safe, open, and in careful order compared with the bulging pigeon-holes of the desk. It was covered with gray powdery film where the police had dusted for fingerprints. The three electric bulbs that had gone off were strung down from the ceiling, one over the desk and two in opposite corners of the room.

"He liked a lot of light."

Carlson nodded. "Had 'em all on tonight. On all over the place when the boys got here, 'cept those three. They came on when they put the fuse back."

He let himself down into the creaking swivel chair. Gus looked at the battered desk against the wall at the front end of the room. It was crowded with papers, the surface as well as the pigeon-holes. A padlock in the middle front hung by a short chain. Behind the desk two long windows were sealed from the inside with brown painted iron shutters. Across them and the strip of wall between them, an old pier-glass, turned lengthwise over the desk, was tilted forward so that Doc Wernitz, sitting there, could glance up and see the whole room—the barred windows at the back end, the brown steel filing cabinet and the open safe blocking the side windows.

"Anything missing, Swede?"

"No idea. You can say in the paper I've only given it a cursory glance, so far."

The chair creaked wretchedly as Carlson leaned back in it. He watched Gus cross the room to read the framed license on the dun-papered wall by the door. It acknowledged receipt of $3,500 and $1 by the Commissioners of Smith County, in return for which they authorized Paul M. Wernitz, operating as The Smith County Recreation Company, Inc., to distribute and offer for rent or lease recreational devices as defined in and in strict accordance with Chapter 482 of the Acts of 1944 and all regulations and amendments thereof. Gus glanced at the official signature at the bottom. It was always a little amusing to him to see Nelson Cadwallader Syms's cramped signature authorizing the distribution and operation of the machines that Aunt Mamie, Mrs. Nelson Cadwallader Syms, girding up her ample loins, was hell-bent on banishing and destroying forever . . . along with one of the County's most lucrative sources of cash income.

There was nothing else in the room to look at except the brown linoleum on the floor, cracked in places and worn to the boards in front of the desk and safe, and two wooden armchairs. There was also a calendar topped with a semi-nude bit of November cheesecake and the compliments of the Smithville Consumers Coal Company. Gus stopped in front of it, studying it with concentrated interest. He was trying to figure out what Swede Carlson was sitting there watching him for. He knew Carlson was a shrewd cop, for all the slow molasses and owl's grease technique, tough and canny, and honest within the pragmatic limits of his calling. At least he had never known him to be dishonest, and he had known him to go out of his way to help people when not doing it would have seemed the smarter tack. Like the Filipino boy waiting outside now—unless that was a little political warfare and Carlson was just seeing to it the County Attorney wasn't making the first arrest. Why, he wondered, was the Swede apparently so interested in him right now? He studied the lady on the calendar a moment longer and turned back.

"Think this is an out-of-county job, Swede? A mob killing?"

It had none of the marks of the two mob killings he'd covered in New York, nor any he'd ever heard about.

Chief Carlson brought the swivel chair creaking back into position. "Might be," he said. "And again it mightn't. I don't know much about it, Gus. Just got here a little before you did—been down in the other end of the county all evenin' talkin' to a guy that knifed his wife. Least that's the way it looks. Looks like a mighty lot of trouble for anybody else to go to."

He got heavily to his feet. "Sort of looks the same way here. But I don't know much about mob killin's, 'cept what I see in the movies when I ain't got my nose to the grindstone, or read about when I got my shoulder off the wheel. When I'm not carryin' the ball, or keepin' my eye on it, that is. Keeps a fella pretty busy, not bein' an acrobat."

Gus grinned at him. "Why does this look the same?"

Chief Carlson glanced bleakly off in the general direction of the kitchen. "Can't say, Gus. Not considerin' the people you're runnin' with here lately."

"—Miss Maynard?" Gus looked at him intently, surprised. "She works on the paper, Swede."

"Sure she does." Carlson agreed amiably. "Come to think of it, her old man owns it.—Used to was, Gus, a fella could tell the *Gazette* somethin' off the record and it was off the record. It's different now. Tell the *Gazette* somethin' and Miss Maynard hot-foots it home and spills it to John. Not that he didn't know it already, mind you, but there were times he didn't know anybody else did. And I'm not sayin' she's out here tonight because he sent her. He's too smart for that."

Gus Blake's gaze was still intent. "If you're saying John Maynard's mixed up with Wernitz——"

"Okay, Gus. He's your boss. Loyalty's a fine thing. All I know is old Doc here gives him a quarter machine for Christmas. Doc Wernitz never gave presents just for fun.—I'll tell you somethin', Gus. When Doc Wernitz told me he was pullin' up stakes and gettin' out of Smith County, he came personally round to Headquarters and took me five miles out on a country road to do it. He didn't want anybody else to know he was pullin' out. He mentioned everybody in general and several in particular he didn't want to know. John Maynard was one of 'em. Funny thing, Gus, you were another."

"Me?" Gus gave him an alerted glance. Then he shook his head. "Unless you mean the editor of the paper."

"No. Not the editor of the paper. He meant you, personally."

"You're nuts, Swede. Or he was. I didn't even know the guy. I made a point of not knowing him." He grinned suddenly. "That's why you've been watching me as if you thought I'd get in the safe?"

"Sure, Gus. One of the reasons."

The bleak eyes rested steadily on him.

"No, I'm goin' to play ball with you, Gus. I'll play ball with you if you'll keep your mouth shut and keep that dame out of this. Hear? Maybe I'm a fool to do it, but I know damn well you didn't slug Wernitz.

Even if it—" Chief Carlson stopped a bare instant, and went on. "—Even if it should look like you might have had some reason to."

Gus Blake looked silently at him. "*Reason* to?"

"Okay, Gus. Keep your shirt on. I'm just a dumb country cop, but there's some things I'd take my Bible oath on. Don't crowd me, now, Gus. If you're in a hole, I'll do my best to get you out. But if I'm wrong— just get this, Gus—if I'm wrong, so help me God I'll hang you higher'n Absalom if I have to do it with my own hands. Now shut up and come on. I want to look around here, and I want to get at that kid out there before that fat-backed County Attorney of John Maynard's throws him in the can and everybody starts yellin' race prejudice. He may be guilty and if he is he's goin' to hang, but till somebody proves it it don't make sense to me."

He kicked the swivel chair toward the desk. "Go on, Gus. Get goin'. I'm lockin' this room up—nobody's goin' to paw around these papers 'cept me. Get all this straight, Gus. I been pushed around longer than I like it. Old Doc here was a sort of friend of mine. See?"

"Sure," Gus said. "I see."

He went over to the door, bewildered to a state of semishock. Either Swede Carlson was drunk or he was, and he knew neither of them was. He had never spoken five consecutive words to the murdered man. He wouldn't have recognized him, dead, down there in the cellar, any more than he would have recognized him alive on Main Street. He tried to think what the man really looked like, alive, without his head caved in and the black spidery veil covering his face. A vague image came into his mind of Doc Wernitz standing alone on the curb in front of the bank in Court House Square at noon one day. Whoever Gus was with had nudged his elbow and said, "That's Doc Wernitz. You know.—Hi, there, Doc. How's tricks?" As the image cleared and focused Gus could see a sort of invisible little man, alone on the curb there, in straight gray topcoat, thick-lensed spectacles, neat-looking in a dry, ageless sort of way, who touched the brim of his gray hat and said, "No tricks." Gus remembered that now, and remembered that hearing him say "No tricks" he'd turned to look at him again, thinking it was a pretty good answer to people who still went on saying "How's tricks," and especially good in Wernitz's line of business.

He could not remember, now, who it was with him, and so far as he could recall that was the last time he'd seen Doc Wernitz until he saw him on the cellar floor, dead as a staved-in mackerel. As for any reason he himself could have . . . The big Swede was bats. He shrugged his shoulders as he crossed the room.

"Or am I bats myself?" he wondered. He went out into the passage and stopped short. Something had happened. When he had first got to the house, and again when he followed Carlson back up from the basement, he'd seen the young cop standing at the foot of the stairs by the Filipino boy who'd found the body. Buzz Rodriguez had been sitting on the stairs, his head in his hands, rocking back and forth, moaning incoherently. Gus had recognized him as one of Wernitz's service mechanics. He'd seen him in a dozen places servicing the fantastically elaborate machines, and sometimes seen him three and four times on a big night at the Sailing Club when the jackpots were falling, come to refill the window and tube of the machines. Something had happened now. The young cop was literally propping Rodriguez against the wall. His face was gray as ashes, his head wobbling forward. Gus turned to Carlson. He was pulling the door of Wernitz's office shut and talking at the same time.

"Get Mac in here to seal this door, Corbin. I'm leavin' the lights on and I want him to sit right here till I get back. Step on it, hear?"

He jerked around to the stairs. The young officer's red face gleamed with sweat. He looked undecided from Carlson to the limp body on his hands.

"Sure, Chief. But this guy's drunk. I don't know——"

Carlson strode across the hall. "What do you mean? This boy don't drink." He picked Rodriguez's slumping body up in one powerful arm, gave him one look and swung around. "Good God, son, this boy's not drunk, he's half dead. Get an ambulance out here. There's a phone in the kitchen—step on it, son. Out there."

He stuck a square forefinger off toward the back of the house. "Upstairs, Gus—get some blankets. This boy's hurt bad. I told that bas——"

Gus cleared the stairs. A door was open at the right. The room there was empty except for an iron folding cot in one corner, but two worn army blankets were folded across the foot. He grabbed them and ran back. Swede Carlson let the boy down on the floor and wrapped him up. His thick fingers moved gently over the back of the boy's head.

"He was slugged too, down there in the basement. Like Wernitz." His face was hard, his colorless eyes set. He got to his feet. "It's a damn good thing I didn't let 'em throw him in the can. He could 'a been dead by mornin'. You would have had a scapegoat." He looked down at Rodriguez, scowling heavily, and went past him to the back of the house. "Mac," he called. "Come in here."

Mac was a short wiry detective in a double-breasted bright blue suit.

"Seal this door up, and watch it. Nobody goes in there. That means nobody." Carlson motioned to the Philippine boy on the floor. "You know Buzz Rodriguez here. When the ambulance comes, Corbin's to go in with him. I'm phoning Stryker to meet him at the hospital and stick with him—all the time. Maybe the kid knows who hit him. I don't want any son of a —— tellin' me he's dead before he can tell it." He put his hand on the door and turned back. "Is there a doctor in Smithville we know don't play the slot machines, Mac?"

The detective went on sealing up the door of Doc Wernitz's room. He shook his head. "Now you know none of them got time to fool around, Chief." He sounded to Gus like a man stepping around a wounded pole-cat on a narrow path.

If Carlson's reply was audible it was not audible to Gus. He followed into the kitchen passage, where a door opened on the cellar stairs.

"—Watch him, Blake." The detective in the bright blue suit spoke cautiously without turning as Gus went by him. "Murders burn him up. Gets mean—meaner'n hell. Get the Maynard girl out of here, if I was you."

Gus quickened his step, and slowed down deliberately. He'd let Connie Maynard off one part of this murder case—the part down in the basement. He knew she was upset anyway. But if experience was what she wanted, she could get the rest of it the way other reporters did and as it came. He grinned without amusement. In front of the cellar door he stopped, listening. Swede Carlson was talking on the phone. "And get hold of Doctor Adams. Tell him it's important, hear?"

The phone went back into place; Carlson was talking to someone in the kitchen. The answer quietly disposed of Constance Maynard, for the time being.

"Outside in her car, Chief. She don't like kitchens, she says. Don't know anything about 'em. She's goin' to wait for Blake."

Carlson came back into the passage. He gave Gus a bleak smile.

"The lady's——"

He stopped as the phone rang. "Hold it, George. I'll answer that." Gus heard him say "Hello," and a silence, and then Carlson's voice again, heavily ironic. "Tell Mr. Maynard Miss Maynard and Mr. Blake are both here. Both doin' nicely. I'll tell Miss Maynard her father's worried about her." He put the phone down and let his breath out slowly. "George, go tell Miss Maynard her father wants her to come home now. Tell her Mr. Blake says he can get along all right from here on without her."

As he came back Gus moved aside for him to open the cellar door. "Watch the old blood pressure, Chief," he said, grinning. "It boils the brains."

"Uh-huh," Swede Carlson said. "Funny thing, when I get blood mad's when I start makin' my big mistakes. I guess that was okay, too. It was a colored boy's voice. I guess John Maynard is anxious, maybe." He took his watch out. "And it ain't late. It's only ten minutes past twelve. She must 'a been out later 'n this several times in her young life."

He opened the cellar door. "Now the rest of 'em are out of the way I want a good look around down here. Comin'? Watch these steps, they're carryin' weight with the two of us."

SIX

CONNIE MAYNARD started violently and whirled around to the man standing in the semidarkness beside her car. She hadn't heard him come out of the kitchen door or cross the yard or seen him till he spoke her name. She shot her hand up to her mouth, stifling an involuntary gasp. He was a policeman. He was saying, "—Miss Maynard." She stared at him in the dim light with a speechless, somehow extraordinary horror.

"Miss Maynard!"

Connie Maynard gripped the wheel tightly. "I . . . I'm sorry!" she said. For one dazed and dizzy instant she had thought the policeman had come for her. She shook her head and pushed her hair quickly back from her forehead. "I'm sorry. I must have been asleep." She hadn't been asleep, unless it was a sort of hypnotic slumber, induced by the darkness all around her, outside and in.

"Your father called up to see if you were still here," the officer said. "Chief Carlson said to tell you Mr. Blake could go in with him. They may be quite a while yet. He says you better go on in."

"Thanks." She had to moisten her lips before she could say it casually

enough. "Tell Mr. Blake I'll wait just the same." She tried to think of
something to add to make it seem amusing if determined, but there was
nothing. She was still too stunned by the effect his appearance had had,
coming just when it did, in the rapidly mounting horror building itself
up in her mind.

"Murder . . . I'd be a murderer too." She was saying that to herself
in the dark recesses of her mind just as he spoke her name, so profoundly
absorbed that his abrupt appearance had made her lose the connection
between herself waiting for Gus out there by herself and seeing them cart
the body away as if it was anything common and ordinary—like the ad
somebody ran in the *Gazette:* Dead Horses Removed. It was sordid and
terrible, and morbid. The whole atmosphere reeked with morbidity and
death. If only she'd insisted on staying inside with Gus . . .

She shot her head up, listening. Somewhere not far away a siren had
begun its low warning whine, rising slowly to a demanding scream,
diminishing again as a twirling red light appeared between the black
cedars lining the dirt lane from the country road. Long yellow fingers
reached out toward the yard. The Fire Department's shining new ambulance streaked past her and pulled up. Two men jumped out. The
policeman who'd told her to go home held the door open for them to
bring the stretcher through. She caught her breath sharply and moved
back, reaching for the chromium arrow on the hood of the car, gripping
it to steady her. An ambulance coming there. . . . She remembered
one of the detectives in the kitchen saying Buzz Rodriguez, the colored
boy, out in the passage, was punch-drunk. But they'd had to call an
ambulance. If somebody called an ambulance for Janey . . .

They were bringing the boy out on the stretcher. She saw Chief
Carlson in the doorway. The young policeman she'd seen in the hall got
in the ambulance behind the stretcher. She didn't see them close the
doors and start off. Gus was there in the doorway with Carlson. The
racing excitement that catching a sudden and unexpected glimpse of
him always built up inside her was there now. She wanted him. If it
weren't for Janey . . . She turned away quickly, biting her lip until the
salt tasted on her tongue. Then she stopped abruptly, suddenly aware
that the ambulance had gone and she was there alone in the yard again,
nothing but silence and the small sounds of the night around her.

She drew a deep breath. *You can't do it, Connie.* No matter how
much she wanted Gus, it was something she couldn't do. It was horrible.
She saw Janey in her mind again, saw her, from halfway along the car-

peted hall, there at her mother's bedside table, with the bottle of pills in
her hand. She saw her resisting them, putting them quickly back, shoving the drawer shut and stepping away. She could have spoken to her
then. She could have said, "Hi, Janey—are you okay?" Or she could
have done it when she saw Janey's body stiffen and saw her twist her
head around on her shoulder and hold it there tightly a moment before
she took a quick step forward, pulled the drawer open, grabbed the
piece of yellow tissue out of the box, picked up the bottle and unscrewed
the top, pouring the capsules into the tissues, twisting the ends together
and thrusting it into her bag.

I should have stopped her then. She whispered it to herself. But she
hadn't. She even smiled, watching her. She put her hand up to her
frozen cheek and rubbed it violently, horror seizing her again. She could
still feel the smile on her face, and the upward tilt of her brow as she
stepped quietly through the open door of her father's room and waited
there, in the dark, until Janey came running out, clutching her bag in
both hands. She could still feel herself standing there, and feel the
satisfied smile that was on her face. She shivered suddenly. It was something evil, hideous, inside her. She'd known it was wrong then, but it
hadn't mattered. Everything was working out perfectly. With Janey out
of the way, everything would be just as she wanted it. But out here alone
in the dark, where she had to stop and sit and listen to the sharp shrill
voice of the conscience she didn't often bother to listen to, it suddenly
mattered. It mattered a great deal.

You can't do it. You get what you want, but you don't get it that way.
Not even her father would approve of that. John Maynard was ruthless
and he was none too scrupulous. She knew that. But this was callousness
—plain and horrible.

She thought of Janey, at home in the narrow brick house, the capsules
in her hand. She wouldn't take them right away. She'd resist them, the
way she'd resisted the impulse to take them from the table drawer.
Connie Maynard moved back to the car. She'd tell Gus, on the way
home. She started to get in under the wheel. Somewhere behind the dark
fringe of trees around the yard something slithered through the dry
grass. A small animal squealed and was silent. There was no sound
except the slithering movement in the grass. Across the darkness came
the high pitch of the siren as the ambulance screamed through Newton's
Corner. Connie tried to swallow. Her throat was as dry as the hard

parched ground under her feet. Maybe she couldn't wait till Gus came
out and she drove him home. Maybe it was too late already . . .

She ran across the yard, catching her foot in a dry rut behind the
green truck, stumbling forward, catching herself again and running on
to the door. "Oh, Gus . . . ?" She pulled the door open. "—Gus,
you've got to go home!" As she stumbled into the kitchen and saw Chief
Carlson and Gus Blake as they whirled around from the passage door,
staring at her, she was conscious that no sound had come from her
throat.

"Connie . . . for God's sake!"

She clenched her fists to control herself.

"Gus—you've got to come home. I'm . . . I'm tired waiting." She
tried desperately to think what she could say. "I'm . . . I'm tired! Do
you hear me? You've got to come home!"

She saw the alarm in Gus Blake's face change as she stamped her foot
on the floor. Anger flashed up in his eyes, his jaw tightened in white
hard ridges. "Gus, please! I'm tired, Gus!"

Then she saw Carlson put his heavy hand on Gus's arm.

"Go on, Gus. It's late. I'm goin' too."

She turned, pushed the door open and ran out again, across the dry
ruts in the littered yard to the safe and cooling darkness of the car.

"Take it easy, son," Swede Carlson said. "High blood pressure boils
the brain. And find out why Miss Maynard's so upset, all of a sudden.
From what I hear, she don't get tired till four or five in the mornin', and
not from just sittin' in a car. Go on, Gus. Maybe we'd both like to know."

The clock in the Court House tower struck eleven as Janey reached
the top of the narrow crooked stairs. She unlatched the folding gate that
was there to keep little Jane from toppling down the steps, fastened it
securely back again and went along the passage to the front room where
she and Gus slept. She switched on the light between the beds, went over
to the dressing table and sat down, looking blindly into the mirror as she
automatically pulled open the side drawer, put her velvet bag into it,
closed it, and reached up and pulled the velvet bow off her hair. After a
moment she got up and went back to little Jane's room, picked up the
warm sleeping child, took her to the bathroom and brought her back,
still half asleep. It was a nightly routine that ordinarily filled her with a
warm glow of happiness. Tonight she went through it automatically,
without feeling. She was too numbed to think or feel.

She put the pink wool panda back up straight in the corner at the foot

of the crib, facing the lop-eared white rabbit in the other corner, saw that
the picture book was on the chair where little Jane could reach it if she
woke first in the morning, and opened the window a little. Out in the hall
she reached up to turn off the light and remembered that Gus never
remembered about the gate across the stairs when he came in late,
always bumped into it, always swore. She left the light on, started back
to her room and stopped. Little Jane had waked.

"Daddy." Janey could hear her voice calling sleepily. "Daddy—little
Dane wants a drink of water." At two and a half she could pronounce all
her letters except the J of her name. Blue-eyed and yellow-haired, she
looked very like what she called herself. Her father called her the little
Dane. The little Dane and the big Swede. It flashed into Janey's mind.
That was what he called the Chief of the County Constabulary. Her
hand trembled as she went back to the girl's door.

"Daddy isn't here yet," she said. "He'll get you a drink of water in the
morning. Good night, sweet."

She heard the sleepy "Night," and closed the door. Her knees were
watery weak again. She put her hand on the rail across the stair well and
stood there. She shouldn't have thought of Chief Carlson. Doc Wernitz's
house was out in the country. The chief of the county police would be in
charge. He'd be out there with Gus now. He was a friend of Gus's. If he
found the checks . . . She closed her eyes, holding on to the railing. It
was all back again, all the writhing agony and despair. A thousand dollars, she thought dully. All the money she'd saved since Gus had turned
over the accounts to her because he could never save anything. She'd
worked so hard, and so gaily, saving it, had such fun shopping and
planning, standing in line at the markets, making her own clothes and
little Jane's, doing everything she knew how to do. Nest egg, back log,
call it anything, money in the bank; something she'd worked so happily
to build up for them, to match the secure enchantment of the other part
of her life with Gus . . . and then turned on, tearing it down and
throwing it away, when Constance Maynard came and she saw all her
dream world dissolving before her. Now, there was nothing left. The
money was gone, the dream was gone. How she could explain it, she had
no idea. She'd destroyed the only thing she'd ever been able to do for
Gus. She wasn't beautiful and brilliant, the way Constance Maynard
was, but she had been practical. She'd made Gus comfortable at home,
and managed, and saved his money so he could buy a new car and have

a new suit and new overcoat, or make a down payment on a house . . . and then she'd turned on him and thrown it all away.

It was all such stupid, sickening folly. And Connie Maynard knew she was stupid. It was in her veiled patronizing smile every time she saw Janey or had to speak to her. And she was right. Gus would be better off with Connie. That was the worst of all of it. *I've failed him in the only thing I knew how to do for him.* . . .

She went back to their room, took off her dress and got her pajamas and yellow wool robe. She put them on, turned down the covers on Gus's bed and hers and sat down, staring at his slippers on the floor. She was dumbly aware, somehow, that if she could get a moment's release from the tension that was blinding her, there might be some way to get out of it. There was none now. She wasn't even thinking straight in her own stupid way; if she had been, she would never have taken the sleeping pills from Mrs. Maynard's table drawer. As they came into her mind again she got up, went to the dressing table, took her bag out of the drawer and reached in it. She touched the gilded lucky piece first, pushed it aside and felt for the folded tissue, to take the pills to the bathroom and flush them down. As they met her fingers, the telephone on the table between the beds jangled noisily.

She thrust the bag quickly into the drawer and shut it, almost as if the phone had eyes to see. As she picked it up, a cold hand closed sharply around her heart. Was it Gus now, calling from out there, to tell her he knew? She let herself sink down on the side of the bed. The phone rang again.

"Hello."

A high-pitched voice, like an old man's whispering, came over the wire. "Is Mr. Blake there?"

"No. He's not in."

"Where is he? Where can I get in touch with him? It's important."

"He's out in the country." She started to say "on the Wernitz case," and didn't. "He'll be here in the morning."

She put the phone down. It was a disguised voice. She knew that without thinking about it particularly. A lot of times people called up in the middle of the night, disguising their voices, to tell the editor of the newspaper something they wouldn't dare tell if there was any chance of their being recognized and held accountable. Usually slander, or . . . She swallowed a bitter doughy lump caught in the middle of her throat.

Was this somebody calling to tell Gus . . . She stood up, took off her robe and laid it across the foot of her bed.

"I've got to stop this," she said softly. "I've got to stop being a fool." She raised the window, got into bed and turned off the light. "I've got to quit even trying to think."

She heard the Court House clock strike the half hour, three quarters, twelve o'clock. Quietly lying there, her mind seemed to clear a little. The thousand dollars was gone. She had to face it, and everything else. There was only one thing to do. That was to tell Gus. She must stay awake, to tell him when he came in. It was all perfectly clear now. She got up, closed the window and opened the hall door. She had to hear him when he came in, and get up and go down and see him downstairs, not up here, where he could fly into a rage and maybe shout at her and wake little Jane. He'd never flown into a rage and never shouted, but he'd never had any reason to before. She shivered a little, not knowing what he'd do, and got into bed again. The quarter hour struck as she lay there staring up at the ceiling.

Then she heard him. Or did she think she'd heard him? She hadn't heard a car drive up. But she wouldn't; he'd drive home with Connie, and leave her and walk home. He wouldn't let her drop him and drive home alone; though she hadn't heard his step on the walk, and he usually ran the last few feet and up the steps onto the porch.

She sat up and turned on the light, listening. Maybe she'd made a mistake. Or she could have heard a rat. Sometimes rats that had been abroad for the summer came back to the old grocery store, not knowing people lived there now. Then she heard his footsteps. He was being very quiet. He usually wasn't. He usually ran into a chair and swore under his breath, the narrow stair well funneling it all plainly up to her on the third floor. Janey wondered a little, now. He must be out in the kitchen, she thought. Always before she'd left coffee for him in the thermos bottle in the pantry, but she had not tonight. Still, there was the coffee cake her mother had made. He could have coffee cake and a glass of milk. She reached for her robe and put her feet in her slippers. She'd go down and see him, and tell him. Now she'd made up her mind, she knew the quicker she did it the better, for everybody and everything. She went out into the hall. Her hands were icy cold, her throat dry and her legs not very steady as she took hold of the rail and leaned over to look down and tell him to wait there.

The light was on in the hall, but he was still out in the kitchen. She

remembered she'd left both lights on when she came up. She took a step
forward and stopped abruptly, looking over the rail down into the hall
again, bewildered suddenly. A door was opening, the door to the basement. She knew its special hinge that whined in spite of all the oil she'd
put on it. He was going, very quietly still, down into the basement. But
he never went down there. He never looked at the furnace, or replaced
a blown fuse, or did any of the things her father did in their basement at
home. She wondered for an instant if he was sick. But that was silly. If he
was sick he'd head for the washroom on the second floor.

She pulled her robe around her, went along to the head of the stairs
and bent down to unlatch little Jane's folding gate. She took hold of the
latch, looking down into the lighted hall. Suddenly there was no light.
She was staring down into pitch and total blackness. The lights had gone
off. There was nothing but darkness thick as a blanket thrown over her
head. She could hear the soft pad of footsteps coming very quietly back
up the basement steps.

SEVEN

THE SOFT PAD of footsteps was coming back up the basement stairs.
Jane swallowed down the great lump swelling in her throat. She moistened her lips and swallowed again. The hinge whined softly and she
heard the muted click of the catch as the door closed. Her legs were
frozen, gripped in an awful paralysis as the blackness crept tighter and
closer around her, suffocating her in its relentless cold invisibility. She
drew herself sharply up and clenched her fists. "No! I'm crazy! There's
no one there. I'm just hearing things. The power's gone off. All over
town. The power's gone off!"

She jerked her head around toward her room and stiffened rigidly
again. The power was not off. She could see the faint greenish glow
change to red, sifting from the street through the closed slats of the
venetian blind at the front window. Her mouth and throat turned dry
again as she turned quickly back, her eyes straining down into the inky
blackness of the stair well. Perhaps it was just their power that had gone
off . . .

Then she heard the loose board in the pantry in front of the dining-room door. Something heavy had touched it . . . something heavier than she was and lighter than Gus. There wasn't a board or step in the house that creaked or a door that opened that she didn't know and couldn't recognize. It was part of the enchanted game she'd played, when Gus had been out at night and she was happily curled up in bed warm and waiting, clocking his progress into the house and through it until he got to the top of the steps and suddenly remembered and started tiptoeing until he got into their darkened room, invariably hitting the foot of his bed, swearing softly until she broke into a laugh. He was always so funny. . . . But this was not funny. The swinging door from the pantry into the dining room was opening. She could hear the soft swish as it scraped its semi-circular pattern across the end of the rug. Her eyes strained wide over the rail, staring down, not sure at first, then horribly sure, with a desperate panic clutching at her heart.

It *was* a light. A faint nebulous glow came seeping, foggy and indistinct, until it focused, brightening, taking form, creeping out of the dining room across the floor into the hall, moving out, onto the rug, rising slowly, like baleful water, up the white baseboard, the nebulous glow sifting between the banister posts, throwing them into wide shadowy bars against the white walls, moving bars as the ball of light moved deliberately forward, deliberate and purposive. It was some one. Some one with a reason. Some one who knew she was there alone. . . . The telephone call. The disguised voice. It flashed into her paralyzed mind with the speed of light, and with the purpose of light, illuminating and clarifying it.

She jerked her body erect, her hands steady and her knees firm and strong. She opened her mouth to scream, to scream and run to the window to scream again. Then she flashed her hand to her mouth and swung around to the door of little Jane's room. She couldn't scream. If she screamed she'd frighten little Jane. Her mind clicked sharply into place as she reached quickly down to the rickety gate, tried it to see it was latched, and turned and ran along the dark passage to her room. If they'd turned off the lights they might have torn out the telephone too— but that she could see, and then, if she had to, she could open the window in front and scream out into the street. She ran around the foot of Gus's bed. Nobody could frighten little Jane. Nobody could come into her house at night and creep around and frighten her child. It was the sort of thing a child might never get over. Her cheeks flushed with sudden anger that burned out all trace of fear. The hand she thrust out reached the telephone accurately. As the dial tone buzzed in her ear her finger flashed around the slots to the last one. Operator. She whirled the dial around and waited, her breath coming quickly.

There was one ring, two rings. She flashed around, looking out into the hall. The soft glow of the light reflected up the narrow shaft of the stairs was brighter. The dark shadow of the rail along the hall was moving, coming closer into focus as the glow reflecting it brightened and came nearer. Janey listened, holding her breath. The corner step where the crooked stairs turned to the second floor had not squeaked. That she would have heard. Then as she did hear it, her heart tightening, the operator's calm voice was in her other ear.

"May I help you?"

"—Call the police. 42 Locust Street. Emergency."

Her voice was crisp and very clear.

"There's some one in the house. The lights are cut off. My child and I are here alone. And call me back quickly. Locust 4298."

"42 Locust Street. Locust 4298. Right."

The operator cut the connection. The dial tone buzzed again in Janey's ear. She slipped the phone quietly back into the cradle, her hand resting on it to pick it up again, her body straight and taut on the side of the bed, her small pointed jaw tight, her hot blue eyes fixed on the foggy glow of light out in the hall. It had stopped. The shadow of the stair rail had stopped moving. It was stationary on the wall. The center board in the hall on the second floor hadn't creaked. But they were close. Too close.

The phone rang sharply. The shadow of the rail jerked and moved crazily up and down for an instant and was fixed and still again. Janey caught the phone up and raised her voice as she said "Hello," turning so it would carry out into the hall and down to the listening ears below. The light moved abruptly and disappeared—into Gus's den. She knew that even before she heard the faint click as the telephone down there was raised and she could hear the sharp breathing of some one else there on the line.

"The police are on their way, Mrs. Blake," the operator's crisp voice said. "The patrol car's at Fifth and Fetter. It ought to be there in less than a minute. I'll call you again. Or why don't I call the people across the street? Who—"

Janey moistened her lips. The downstairs phone had gone quietly back into place. The quickly drawn breath was no longer there in her ear. The light was in the hall again. The shadow of the rail flew up to the white wall and was blotted out as the light below faded and disappeared as silently as it had come.

"No," she said. "Don't bother. I . . . I think he's gone. But you'd better call again."

She put the phone down. The police were coming. Maybe Gus would come with them, she thought. It flashed into her mind that that was silly. Gus was with the county police. It was the city police coming here to her. County and city police weren't the same at all. She went quickly over to the window and drew up the blinds. There was a little light outside, light in relation to the pitchy blackness inside the house. She crept back quickly into the hall and stood leaning over the rail, looking down. There was no sound, nothing. Then abruptly she heard a sound. It was the oil burner. She heard it switch on and heard the familiar tap-tap-tap, like little ghosts playing hop-scotch up and down the hot water pipes as it started to work. She stood there, listening. After a long moment she let her breath out and drew it in again slowly. It meant that a door or window had been opened and cold air was coming into the house. The thermostat was set at 60. She listened still. The oil burner was still going. Then there was another tap-tap, louder than that the little ghosts made in the pipes. She turned and ran to the front window and threw it up. She leaned out. A car with lights dimmed was at the curb. A dark uniformed figure was at the end of the walk, another at the front door, knocking on it.

"I'll come down," she called.

"You stay there, ma'am, till we get in. We've got the house surrounded."

It did not sound stilted or absurd to Janey. It sounded wonderful.

"Okay. I think it must be the back door. The switch is in the basement."

She closed the window and went back into the hall. In a moment she heard heavy honest feet on the first floor and saw bobbing lights with a nebulous glow that held no terror. She unlatched the gate and tied her robe more securely around her as she felt her way down the stairs. She was halfway down to the first floor when the lights flashed on. The policeman standing by the front door stared at her. He thrust his gun back into the holster.

"You could 'a got shot easy, lady," he said irritably. "I told you to stay up there."

Janey came on down the stairs. She drew herself up with dignity. "I don't want my little girl waked up," she said stiffly. "I don't want people tramping all over the house waking her up."

The policeman stared at her. "Look, lady. You don't seem to realize—" He stopped. "Okay, Mrs. Blake. I guess you scared him away. The back door's open. I'll have a look all around upstairs. You go in there and sit down. I won't wake your girl up."

Janey went into the dining room, switched the lights on and sat down. She was sitting there, the sapphire sparks still shooting from her wide blue eyes, when he came back again.

"All okay upstairs, Mrs. Blake. Are you all right?"

Janey nodded.

"If you're alone here, I'll leave a man——"

"You don't have to do that," Janey said quickly. "I'm sure he won't come back. My husband will be home pretty soon. We'll be perfectly all right. I'm not scared. I . . . I was at first, but then I . . . I was just mad, I guess."

He hesitated, looking at her sitting there. You wouldn't think she had that much of what it takes. Mosquito weight, plenty of punch.

"All right, Mrs. Blake. You'll be all right. You go to bed and go to sleep. We'll keep an eye out. Will you leave a note for your maid not to touch anything down there around the fuse box, and tomorrow we'll dust that switch for fingerprints."

"I don't have a maid," Janey said.

"Okay, then, Mrs. Blake. I'll lock up in back for you and go out the front door. Tomorrow morning Lieutenant Williams'll want to talk to Mr. Blake about this. Can you see he's here round nine-fifteen? And you ought to get him to put a bolt on your kitchen door. Any dime store key'll open it."

He was back in an instant. "Good night, Mrs. Blake."

"Good night."

She waited for him to close the door, still very calm. The closing of the door shattered all her control as instantly as if it had been a rainbow bubble hitting the floor, bursting into a million pin points of soapy water.

"Oh, no!" She gripped the edge of the table. She could hear heavy steps coming along the side of the house. They were all going, leaving her alone again. She ran to the front door, her heart in her throat, and stopped, the tears pricking like hot grease along her eyelids. She backed away from the door and went back into the dining room, sank down into the chair and put her head down on her arms. She raised it again quickly, listening. It was nothing but the icebox coming on. She listened again. The Court House clock struck one. She looked at the clock on the thermostat by the door. One o'clock. Only one o'clock. If only Gus would come . . . if he'd only come home. At least he'd be proud of her for keeping her head, and not screaming and frightening the little Dane. She put her head down on her arms on the table for a moment to rest before she sat up to take up her vigil in the quiet night again.

EIGHT

IT WAS ten minutes past two by the clock on the elegant simulated tortoise-shell dashboard and five minutes past by the clock on the Court House tower as Connie Maynard flipped the wheel lightly around and turned out of the Square into Fetter Street.

"I tell you again, Gus," she said patiently, "There's nothing whatever wrong with me. No matter what Swede Carlson thinks or you or anybody else thinks. I just got a case of jitters, sitting out there alone."

Now that she was back in town, among houses and people who were alive, not dead, she was ready to believe that was the way it was. It had all been a sort of wild phantasmagoria that didn't make any possible sense. She ought never to let anything like a conscience bother her. All a conscience was was an atavistic throwback to childhood, your own and your family's, when you were taught a lot of nonsense and punished if you didn't follow it. Janey wasn't going to take any sleeping pills. That was nonsense of another sort. More of her old broken-wing tactics.

"I got the most awful jitters out there, Gus, and I'm terribly ashamed of myself. Will you excuse it, please? Just this once, please?"

That was the line to take. She realized it instantly, aware of the change taking place in him as he relaxed a little in the seat beside her. There was no use being stiff-necked and combative, the way she'd started out being. It only made him more and worse of both. She ought to know him well enough by now to know that if nothing else.

"I'm really horribly sorry, Gus. Please, don't be cross with me. I guess I'm not nearly as competent as I try to pretend. I guess murder's something you have to get used to, isn't it?"

"It sure is," Gus said. He knew it from a lot of experience. He was sick out behind a row of garbage cans the first one he'd covered. Even if she didn't see Wernitz on the cellar floor, she'd sat out in the dark and seen them take him away, and seen the ambulance. Imagining things was a lot worse sometimes than seeing them. "It's my fault," he said. "I shouldn't have let you go."

"Oh, then you're not mad at me, Gus? Thanks! You're sweet. May I kiss you? Do you mind if I do, Gus—just once?"

She leaned over toward him, the car swerving with the quick movement of her body.

"Drive, Connie. Drive the car and keep off the milk truck."

They weren't quite on it, but they would be if Connie got her libido all unleashed, which usually happened when she got contrite and feminine. "And don't make passes at your boss." He grinned at her in the dark. She laughed and slowed the car down for the red light.

"Who's going to make them if I don't?" she inquired easily. "Marriage has made you horribly stuffy, hasn't it? Or are you just afraid to let yourself go?"

The light changed. Instead of turning left toward her own house, she turned toward the center of town.

"Hey," Gus said, "Where—"

"Who's driving this car, Mr. Blake?" She kept to the right and down Locust Street. "I took you out, and I bring you back. The Maynard shuttle service has its standards."

"Don't be a dope, Con. I don't want you to drive out alone. I don't care about you, but your father'll be sore. It's after two."

A smile moved in her yellow-green eyes. Something was finally working the way she'd planned it—planned and forgotten it in her sudden attack of moral jitters out in the Wernitz yard. She'd planned it on her way in to pick him up and take him out to Wernitz's, as part of her cold war against Janey. Janey would be awake and watching, she was sure of that. She'd probably be upstairs in the dark, looking out the window, and she'd see her drive Gus up to the door. Gus would have to object to her going back by herself—as a supper guest at her father's house that night, he'd have to object. And Janey would see them drive up, and drive off again. And it was working. The house was just a block away now. She let him protest until suddenly she was aware that something wasn't working.

"Oh, my God!" she thought. Her hand on the wheel tightened. The car lurched a little and came back as she caught herself and it. Something had gone wrong. Her mouth was as dry again as it had been out in the Wernitz yard. A policeman . . . More alert for the sight of the narrow red brick house behind the privet hedge at the moment than Gus, who turned, telling her to drive on around the block and he'd take her home and get a taxi back, she'd seen the uniformed policeman come up and turn in there. Gus had not. She'd seen the lights in the house first too, in the dining room downstairs, in the living room on the second floor and bedroom on the third. "—Oh, no, she couldn't have!" But why were the lights on at a quarter past two, and why was the policeman going into the house? Connie moistened her parched lips. *She must have done it.*

It was an instant of impulsive dismay not as close to horror as she had thought it was going to be, or as it had been out in the dark yard. Here in town, with Gus beside her, a *fait accompli* almost in her hands, she was herself again. She was the girl slipping back into the shadow of her father's room, watching Janey, pleased that Janey was taking the sleeping pills from her mother's table drawer. She could feel the hard tight smile on her face again there in the car. It *was* what she wanted. She'd been a stupid fool out at Wernitz's.

"What goes on?" Gus said suddenly. He'd turned to look at the house. It was surprise that alerted him, nothing more. He wasn't worried, only surprised to see the house all lighted up at a quarter past two in the morning. "Better stop."

Connie Maynard had already decided that. Her foot was on the brake and she was slipping easily along the curb.

"Maybe Janey's—" She started to say maybe Janey was sick, but that was a mistake. She realized abruptly that with the scene she'd made out in the country, and even in spite of her denials there was anything behind it, it could look very strange. "Maybe Janey's got company— strays from our party." She said it lightly as she stopped the car. The fact that there were no cars except Gus's old coupé in front of the house occurred to her at once. "Or maybe just Orvie," she said. "Let's both go in, shall we? Maybe there's a cup of coffee. Or I could even do with a drink, after what I've been through—or what you've been through with me."

"Okay." Gus opened the door and held it while she slid across the seat and out at the brick walk. He was looking up at the house, a little worried, she thought, in spite of what she'd said. Worried about the kid, probably, she decided as he closed tne door. She went up the walk with him, her pulse beating quickly, her throat dry, not with any agonized remorse, but dry the way it was at the races or when she saw Gus suddenly come into a room. She held her breath sharply as he put his key in the lock, turned it and pushed open the door. And let it go as sharply as she stepped inside and looked around. The policeman? Where had he got to? There was no one in the hall, and no one moving upstairs. She was listening intently to hear them up there. Then she turned and looked into the lighted dining room. Gus had shut the door and come on in. He was there in the double door beside her. Both of them were looking at Janey, in her yellow wool dressing gown, her head on her folded arms, her eyes closed, her long lashes sweeping her pale cheeks, asleep, quietly asleep. Connie's heart leaped for an instant.

"Why, she's asleep." Gus said it in the surprised way people say unexpected obvious truths.

Connie stood motionless there. Her eyes, moving around the room, fell suddenly on a small bright orange capsule, on the floor against the table leg. She moved a step to hide it from Gus. Her hands were trembling. Then she had taken them. . . . She looked quickly back at Janey, aware that Gus had moved. He was going over to the table.

"Why don't you just let her sleep, Gus, till she wakes up?" Connie Maynard said. "She doesn't look as if she'd had much sleep lately, does she?" She went close to the table herself, bent down quickly and picked up the orange capsule, slipped it into her coat pocket.

"No, I'll get her upstairs."

As she spoke, Janey stirred and opened her eyes. "Gus!"

She got up quickly. "Oh, Gus!" She put her hands out to him, and saw Constance Maynard. She dropped her hands to her sides and took a step forward.

"Janey, what's happened? What the—" Gus stopped and began again. "Janey, what's the matter?"

"—Just waiting for you, dear," Connie said. She stifled a slight yawn. "It is frightfully late, of course. But now we're here what about a drink?" She looked at Janey. "Or do you want to go to bed? Don't mind me if you do. I'll swallow it down and scoot along. I wish newspaper offices closed down on Saturday." She turned to Gus. "What about a drink, boss? And don't look at Janey like that. A girl's got a right to wait up for her husband. And it's her dining room, isn't it? I mean if she likes to sleep sitting up. . . ?"

"Shut up, Connie." He cut her off brusquely. She knew she was making him sore, but that was all right. If he was sore at her he wouldn't be too patient with Janey. That was the point right now. No man, especially not Gus Blake, liked the idea of a woman waiting up for him, especially when another woman was a witness to it.

"What's the idea, Janey?" he asked impatiently.

Connie's eyes smiled. She was so right. And Janey was such a little sheep. All she did was open her vapid blue eyes a little wider, move back another step, take hold of the back of the chair and moisten her pale lips.

"If I ever wait up for him," Connie thought, "I won't have on cotton pajamas and a woolen bathrobe, and I'll comb my hair and put on some lipstick. And I won't let him push me around like this."

"Nothing's the matter, Gus," Janey was saying. "I . . . I guess I just went to sleep, is all." She turned her small white face to him and tried to smile. "I'm sorry you caught me. Why don't you get Connie a drink? There's some scotch in the pantry. And then take her home."

"That's big of you, madam," Connie said pleasantly. "But I can get home with no trouble whatsover. I would like a drink."

"I'll get you one if you two dames will shut up."

Gus pushed a chair into the table, pushed open the pantry door and let it swing shut.

"You know the green-eyed business is frightfully young, Janey," Constance Maynard said evenly. "Did you drop this? I found it here on the floor." She took the orange capsule out of her pocket and held it out to Janey. She smiled again. The girl really had thought of taking them tonight. She could tell by the way her body stiffened and her saucer eyes opened even wider. "Take it, dear. It's yours. You don't have to worry. It takes guts to really go to sleep."

She felt Janey's cold finger tips touch her hand as she silently took the capsule and put it in the pocket of her dressing gown. She started almost convulsively as Gus pushed the pantry door open again.

"Didn't your mother stay, Janey?" he asked. Connie's eyes smiled again. He was the picture of the intelligent male trying to find out what was going on in the minds of a couple of women, one acting true to form, the other off on a tangent that made no sense of any kind.

"Oh, if she did then you can take me home, can't you?" Connie said quickly. "I do really hate to go alone." She took the highball he handed her, raised it to her lips and smiled across the rim of it at Janey.

"Is your mother here?" Gus asked impatiently. "I told you—"

Janey found her voice. "Yes. She's here. She's upstairs." Her fingers tightened on the back of the chair. "I've made up the couch in the study for you. And if you . . . if you don't mind, I'll go on up and go to bed. Good night. Good night, Connie."

NINE

THE IRON CURTAIN would be fluttering in as many shreds as a grass skirt if the news of the world spread as fast and as pervasively as local gossip in Smithville. It dripped from the sable wings of night and sped forth refreshed on the golden wings of the morn. On Saturday morning everybody in Smithville was feeling exceedingly sorry for Janey Blake. Her overdraft varied from one hundred to one thousand dollars, but there was no variation in the reason for it: the slot machines, the way Gus Blake was carrying on, tearing around the country with John Maynard's divorced daughter. Even after Janey had driven a burglar out of the house single-handed, Gus Blake had come home and brought the Maynard girl with him and gone off with her again, not getting back till five o'clock in the morning, leaving little Mrs. Blake and the kid alone there in the house all night. It made the patrolman watching the house sore as a pup. It was a dirty trick, with Mrs. Blake scared as she was and pretending she wasn't. The milkman who saw Miss Maynard kissing Gus Blake at two o'clock in the morning on Fetter Street didn't care what they did if she hadn't nearly run into his truck just as he was starting out. They could kiss each other all they pleased—what worried him was five hundred bottles of milk and cream and an undetermined amount of cottage cheese. And everybody felt exceedingly sorry for Janey. Everybody, with two exceptions. One was Constance Maynard, who still, however, in a way and when she didn't stop to think, felt a little sorry for Janey, in the slightly contemptuous and offhand way a beautiful sleek panther might feel about a young sheep she was trailing across an open field of daisies.

The second exception was the murderer of Paul M. Wernitz.

There was nothing in all this that made Smithville very different from any other town. Gus Blake was finding that out daily as he tried to make it sound unique and interesting for the Centennial edition of the *Gazette*.

Nor was domestic conversation very different, even in the homes of the people who had been to the Maynards' party the night before and had to be at the office the same time Saturday morning as they were the other five working days of the week.

Martha Ferguson, the red-haired wife of the president of Smithville's leading bank, pulled the plug out of the coffee pot and glanced up, past her red-haired freckle-faced thirteen-year-old daughter, earnestly frying bacon and eggs, at the clock on the back of the electric range. It was ten minutes past eight, and Jim was still not down. Fortunately her son did not have to shave yet, and a bath, so far as she knew, had never taken him more than three minutes except under compulsion since he'd graduated from outside assistance. He was over at the sink, in as much of his football gear as was permitted by the house rules, diluting the frozen orange juice. Martha Ferguson put two more slices of bread in the toaster.

"I don't know what on earth's keeping your dad this morning," she said. "The Maynards' hoedown certainly doesn't account for it. We were home by twelve." She waited for the toast to pop up, took it out and buttered it. "Do you people realize," she said, "that all over the United States there are people just like us, waiting for the man of the house to get out of the bathroom and come down and eat? Millions and millions of them. Anybody that thinks the bathroom in the American home is a sanitary device is nuts. It's nothing but a throwback to the prehistoric cave where the male could hide in comfort in his fur skins while the female and the young were outside in the cold hunting sticks to rub together. And if you spill much more of that orange juice, sweetie, there won't be any left."

She laughed at her son and went out into the hall.

"Jim, are you ever coming down? What on earth are you doing? If you're eating soap, there's bacon and eggs down here. You've got to get to the bank. You're only president of it—you don't own it."

"Coming, darling." Jim Ferguson, hurrying down from the landing, stopped to check his pockets for handkerchief, billfold, change and fountain pen. She waited for him at the foot of the stairs.

"—Do something about those checks of poor little Janey today, Jim." She spoke earnestly, lowering her voice so the children could not hear her. "I simply can't bear to think of her going around with all this hanging over her. Can't we lend her the money to cover the things, Jim? I could get it from Dad. He might just as well loosen up a bit before he dies. I'll write to him today. But for heaven's sake, come and eat."

At the Nelson Cadwallader Syms' house in Bateman Street, Connie Maynard's Aunt Mamie Syms towered like the chairman of the Committee of the Whole at the head of the heavy empire table in the old-fashioned dining room, where militant pieces of family furniture stood about against the brown papered walls as if they had waited too long to march out and at last had given up hope. The dust of Aunt Mamie's tenure had faded off their spit and polish into an adamantine gray except on the surface portions that even Aunt Mamie's down-at-the heel maid couldn't overlook. As the long narrow windows were seldom washed and were hung with sun-faded brown rep curtains, it was hardly noticeable, and Aunt Mamie's vigorous attention was fixed on civic, not domestic, problems. Except at the moment. She took off her reading glasses and put down her paper.

"Dorsey," she said.

Aunt Mamie's son was older than Martha Ferguson's, and instead of a football jersey and simulated Notre Dame pants he wore a chalk-stripe blue suit, a blue shirt and blue-striped tie. He was already through his breakfast, waiting for another cup of coffee, the only product of the Syms kitchen that could be called even average.

"Dorsey." Aunt Mamie tapped the table with a wing of her horn-rimmed glasses that were as near a gavel as anything at hand. "*Where is your father?*"

Dorsey Syms turned the Maynard brown eyes and the Maynard smile toward his mother as he put down the sporting and financial section and pushed his plate back. He didn't answer. Aunt Mamie's questions were mostly rhetorical, or, if not rhetorical, fully capable of being, and intended to be, answered from the chair.

"I hope," Aunt Mamie said, glancing toward the clock on the big empire sideboard, "that he hasn't forgotten he's supposed to look over the letter I've written. Gus Blake tampered with the last one I wrote. I can spell quite as well as any one else. I was deeply mortified, the way it came out in the paper. Your father's just dawdling, this morning—dawdle, dawdle."

Dorsey smiled at her. She'd forgotten she was late for breakfast herself. No one, however, could ever accuse her of dawdling.

"And just when I've got to see Doctor Mason," his mother added. "I have a very severe headache. It must be my eyes."

Only a stout effort on the part of a stout woman kept Aunt Mamie
from putting her head on her hands and all three on the breakfast table.
Dorsey smiled again and looked at his watch.

"Why don't you just wait, Mother?" he said. "Maybe it'll wear off.—
I mean, you don't have to use your eyes much today or tomorrow.
Maybe they'll clear up if you rest them a little. You do too much."

"Well, perhaps, Dorsey."

He heard his father coming slowly down the stairs. He pushed his
chair back. It was a dirty trick, going off, leaving his father to cope with
one of his mother's champagne eyestrains. But there'd be a lot to do at
the bank this morning. There were at least ten people in town who'd
hotfoot it there as soon as they opened their morning mail. Which meant
work for him in the savings department. The ones who had savings
would have to take them out. The others . . . Dorsey Syms shrugged
mentally. That was their problem. Old Doc Wernitz must have had some
wry sense of humor, he thought. Maybe he got a kick out of hanging on
to a lot of checks people wrote after their sixth highball and forgot about.
Maybe he'd really enjoyed bringing them all in in one batch, just toward
the holidays and at the end of the month, when most Smithville bank
accounts were on their last legs anyway. Notices had gone out to ten
depositors, six with savings. An eleventh should have gone to Janey
Blake. But it hadn't. And there was no telling how many the other two
banks across Court House Square had sent out.

He listened to his father coming along the hall. His father banked
over at the Merchants National. It was the one determined stand Dorsey
had ever known Nelson Cadwallader Syms to make. He'd refused, even
in face of the plea of family solidarity, to bank where his wife's brother
John Maynard was on the Board of Directors. Poor old Nelly, Dorsey
thought. He was probably expecting a notice himself that morning, and
was in no hurry of any kind to get to the office to get it.

Dorsey went around the table and dropped a kiss on his mother's
feverish cheek. "I've got to rush," he said. He raised his voice to carry
to the hall. "So long, Dad. I've got to shove. See you later." He went out
the other way, through the kitchen. He always hated to see his father
beaten down.

The butler at the Rogers' country house out on the Bay glanced apprehensively at the paper propped up in front of the master of the house
at the foot of the dining table. Mr. Rogers had cleared his throat twice

already. The third time was the boiling point, in caloric inverse to the bacon and eggs under the plastic lid covering Mr. Orval's plate at the other end of the table. The butler's palms were discreetly moist as he listened intently for Mr. Orval to burst out of his room upstairs. He could hear him then, running halfway down the stairs and slowing up to come the rest of the way quietly and soberly. Mr. Orval's father did not like people being late to meals and having to race into the dining room, no matter how many parties they'd been to the night before. The butler cleared his own throat noiselessly and breathed more freely as he poured a cup of coffee from the silver pot and put it at Mr. Orval's place.

"Good morning, sir," he said.

Mr. Rogers' gray brows beetled over the edge of his paper, but not before Orvie Rogers had had time to give his tie a yank into proper place.

"Good morning, son."

"Good morning, Dad."

Mr. Rogers went back to his paper, Orvie took the lid off his bacon and eggs.

The butler glided across the thick Chinese rug through the swinging door into the pantry as Mr. Rogers cleared his throat the third time Behind the door he paused, listening discreetly. He wondered just how rough a session it was going to be. Mr. Orval was not any too fit. The expression on his face as he'd lifted the plastic lid had nothing to do with the bacon and eggs being cold. It had to do merely with their being. He heard Mr. Rogers clear his throat again.

"About those checks we were talking about, son."

The butler glided swiftly away toward the kitchen. He had heard Mr. Rogers discuss checks with his son before at breakfast, and it was nothing he cared to listen to again.

"You'll find a check on my desk, Orvie," Mr. Rogers said. "I want you to take it by and give it to Janey. Tell her it's a personal loan from me to her, and she can pay it back when and as she can."

Orvie Rogers looked up quickly and opened his mouth. He closed it again as his father cleared his throat for the fifth time. "I understand this fellow Wernitz was murdered last night."

"So I heard," Orvie said. Even coffee tasted foul this morning.

"Good riddance. I wish we could get those machines out of Smith County. Nobody would think of cutting a hole in his pants pocket to let his money dribble out, and nobody with any gumption would put a nickel in a coin machine."

His brows beetled over at Orvie again. He knew Orvie played the slot machines, and Orvie knew he knew it.

"In any case," he said, "Janey's a fine girl. I don't want her mixed up with this filth. I'm very fond of Janey."

He said it very much as if it were a personal accusation. Orvie waited, half expecting, from long experience, that his father would go on and say, "If you'd had the gumption of a wet muskrat you'd have married her before Blake did." He didn't mind it any more. Things would have been different if he had married her . . . or if she would have married him.

"And I suggest you let Blake get out of the way before you go there," his father said. "I've got some idea that what Gus doesn't know about this won't hurt him. I dare say most of us are fools when we get out of our own field. I learned that when we had to convert the plant at the beginning of the war."

At John Maynard's house in town his daughter, in a tailored suit and white blouse tied in a flat bow at the neck, ready for a day's work at the *Smithville Gazette,* jabbed viciously into the grapefruit in front of her as she waited for her father's footsteps on the stairs. At last she put her spoon down impatiently and pressed the bell under the table. When the colored boy came she said, "Lawrence—go upstairs and find out what in God's name is keeping my father. Bang on the door. Maybe he's slipped in the shower."

She picked up her spoon again. "Never mind. Here he comes."

She raised her voice. "Daddy, if you don't hurry you're not going downtown with me."

Then she realized that he was not coming. He was going into the library first. She looked at her watch. She was in a hurry. Gus always got to the office earlier than anybody else, and she had some unfinished business with Gus that she wanted to get on with. Her father was coming now. She looked up expectantly at him. Then she frowned. He wasn't smiling his slow easy smile, as he usually did. "What's the matter, Daddy?"

"Nothin', honey."

John Maynard came around the table and kissed her on the top of her head. He went to his place at the end of the table, waiting until the colored boy had gone out of the room.

"Connie, you haven't done anythin' foolish, have you, honey?" he asked gently.

"Lots of things, I guess, Dad. Why? What particular one do you want to know about now?"

"I'm not jokin', honey. I'm talkin' about those checks I showed you last night. Did you take 'em out of the drawer in there?"

Connie Maynard stared at him. "Good heavens, no. Why should I do that? They're not—do you mean they're gone?"

"That's what I mean, Con. They're gone. The whole lot of 'em. I was goin' to take 'em around after Gus left home this mornin' and have a little talk with Janey." He looked past her out of the window for a few moments. "I'm tryin' to think who was in there last night.—Who'd want to take 'em, I mean, Connie."

He shrugged and picked up his napkin, the old smile coming back on his handsome rugged face. "It was mighty nice little Janey won the jackpot last night."

Connie was watching him intently across the table.

"Daddy," she said sharply. She put down her coffee cup. "Just how well did you know this Doc Wernitz who was killed last night?"

John Maynard smiled at her. "Now, honey." He wiped his broad mouth with the corner of his napkin. "Now, honey . . . if I was you, I'd just keep my little nose out of things that don't concern me. It's always best. Usually I've always found it was safest, in the long run, too."

TEN

THE MURDERER of Paul M. Wernitz mentally shook his head a little. It was a mistake to come down later than usual for breakfast. It was a mistake to do anything to call anybody's attention to the fact that he wanted time to be alone, to think, to calculate and reflect over his errors, so he could retrieve them if necessary and guard against future ones. Above all, he had to act as if there was nothing special on his mind, act as normally and casually as he always acted. He had to forget the sound of old Wernitz's head as the iron bar hit it, not a loud sound, more like an eggshell as you closed your hand on it to crush it. But that was not why he'd spent so much time over his bath and

shave. It was the unfortunate fact that in the average house the bathroom was the only place a man could lock the door and be alone without the risk of somebody walking in and surprising some expression
that the most astute and carefully guarded mind might transmit unconsciously to the motor nerves and impulses controlling any man's
face. He had seen something of it in his own face in the medicine chest
mirror as he thought about himself, and the mistakes he'd already
made, when he was wiping his face after he had rinsed off the shaving
soap. But it wasn't Wernitz's eggshell skull he had been thinking about.
He kept his eyes down on his plate as he thought about it all again.

"Damn Janey Blake," he said quietly to himself. Who would ever
have thought the little devil had that much guts? If he hadn't had the
quick-wittedness to pick up the phone in Gus's den they might easily
have got him. But they still wouldn't have been able to connect him
with the Wernitz thing out at Newton's Corner. That was the one
thing he didn't have to worry about. He had been too smart to leave
any tracks behind him there. He frowned suddenly, and bit his lower
lip, remembering he was supposed to appear as he always did. He relaxed and took up his coffee cup, took a swallow and put it down
calmly.

The Janey business was an error. He could see that now. Calling her
up, and calling up out at Wernitz's to check on Gus and Connie, had
seemed to make it easy going. It wasn't his fault she turned out to be
so quick on the trigger, but it was the sort of thing he should have been
smart enough to figure on.

"I can't afford any more mistakes," he thought. Janey was his second, or third. No. His fourth. He had to be brutally honest with himself
if nobody else. He had to see his mistakes and admit them, and above
all not miss any of them.

"It's a funny kind of thing," he thought, moving the newspaper so
it shielded his face. It wasn't as if he'd acted on the spur of the moment. He'd known for some time he was going to kill Paul M. Wernitz.
He had considered ways and means on what he might call an academic
level for quite a while. The fact that Wernitz had forced his hand by
suddenly letting it be known he was closing up shop and leaving Smithville, so that he had to use perhaps his least brilliant modus operandi,
was unfortunate in one sense but very fortunate in another. Brilliance
was likely to be involved, while in a murder at least simplicity and the
presence of a natural and obvious suspect—especially if he happened

to be an alien employee—was all to the good, if not egotistically so satisfying. He had been surprised himself at how neat the whole thing was . . . just as he was surprised now at how easy it was to carry on as if there was nothing at all on his mind. He heard himself listening and talking as much as he ever talked while he was trying to read the paper at the breakfast table. It was almost as if he were two people existing in one body. The only thing to watch, really, was that one didn't get confused with the other.

He turned the page of the paper, realizing that the page he was apparently so engrossed in had nothing on it but an ad for a special sale of women's fur coats. He turned to the financial reports. That was something he could be legitimately engrossed in, if anybody happened to notice.

Janey was a mistake. But Janey was only secondary, an effect following a cause, and the cause was his real mistake. "It was just a piece of damned luck, is all it was," he told himself. But it wasn't true, and he knew it. If he had let the blasted thing stay where it was, he wouldn't have had any bad luck to complain about. Up to that point, everything was okay. Nobody could trace the calls he put in to get the service mechanics out of the place and off to the farthest corners of the county. He'd figured them out with a map, and gone to each place, to see for certain that Wernitz owned the machines there, get the names of the people who'd call in, and even listen to them to see what they'd say when they did call. He'd made a mistake about Heron Point, not checking up to find out it was closing down the day before. But even that had worked out all right too, because Buzz Rodriguez who took the call hadn't remembered either, until he was halfway there, so that he got to the basement only in time to get a crack on his head too. All that, with the one slight mistake that hadn't mattered, had been carefully worked out and skillfully done.

The thing to do now was to sit tight; and there was one little trouble. He frowned down again at the small print of the stock market listings before he could catch himself. He had to get the thing he'd made the stupid mistake, his only serious mistake, of picking up off the dirt floor of Wernitz's cellar.

"—I don't know why the hell it worries me the way it does." He could say that again, the way he'd said it to himself when he'd almost nicked his jawbone shaving. The chances were a hundred to one, a thousand to one more likely, that nobody but himself knew anything about it, or could even connect him with Wernitz by means of it. Wernitz was close-mouthed, solitary in a psychotic degree. Afraid of the dark, blinding himself with glaring white lights, superstitious as a root-and-clay painted aborigine clutching on to his tribal talisman. But a talisman lost potency if other tribesmen knew about it. Even Achilles probably never went around bragging about his heel.

He quit reading the market reports and took another swallow of coffee. It was cold now, but he hardly noticed it. The palms of his hands had broken out in cold sweat. He unobtrusively wiped them off on the napkin in his lap. A hundred to one or a thousand to one, he had to get Wernitz's talisman back, the gold-washed lucky quarter that he could have known Wernitz would reach for when the lights went off, to hold in his hand to come down into the shadow-filled basement and put in a new fuse. It must have been in his hand, to fly out and land, glittering like an evil eye there on the dirt floor when the iron bar came down on the eggshell skull.

"Why did I have to pick it up? Why didn't I leave it there?"

He knew the answer to that too. It had appealed to a kind of grizzly sense of ironic relief, all of a sudden. It had even been grimly comic. "Who ever called this thing a lucky piece?" Wernitz had been almost fanatically dependent on it.

He took the last bite of his toast and the last sip of cold coffee. It was entirely by accident he'd learned about it himself. Some perfectly minor and unimportant piece of business that needed Wernitz's signature. He had said Yes, in the clipped laconic way of speaking he had, and then put his hand in his pocket, taken something out, put it on the table under his hand and peered at it. He said Yes again. Then, as he'd started to put it back in his pocket his elbow struck the chair and the thing fell on the floor. He went after it in a flash. It was the gilded quarter. Funny, all of it, in one way, but not in another. Not the way Wernitz's dry face had broken out with sweat as he retrieved it and put it back in his pocket. "No," he said then. "I don't sign." And he didn't. "Bad luck," he said. That finished it. And as a matter of fact it had turned out that way. He'd been right for whatever wrong reason.

And now the thing had dropped on another floor. If he believed in bad luck he might well break out into sweat again. He wiped his palms again on his napkin, though there was no need to. He was a damn fool for ever picking it up off the dirt floor, a worse fool for putting it in his trousers pocket just for the ironic devil of it—as well as to have it where nobody cleaning his desk or dresser drawer might come across it and wonder—but the worst stupidity of all was forgetting it and reaching in his pocket and dropping it in the slot machine . . . and never thinking about it until it came rolling along across the floor until Connie put her foot out and stepped on it.

"I should have got hold of it then," he thought. He could easily have done it. If, in fact, he had simply said "That's mine" nobody would ever have thought of it a second time. Instead, it had suddenly seemed a good idea to be rid of it, get it away from him so he wouldn't make another mistake of the same kind. It wasn't until it was in Janey's bag—or not even then, not until she burst into tears and was running past him up the steps—that he realized if the hundred-to-one chance came through it was the only thing that could tie him to Wernitz's house and the Wernitz murder.

His palms were clammy and moist again.

"I've got to get it." As he got up from the breakfast table he knew that as clearly as he knew the sun was shining outside and that Paul M. Wernitz was dead, in the infinite darkness of eternity. Not that he was superstitious, even if the thing did seem suddenly imbued with a malignant animate perversity all its own. Otherwise how had it got into the tube or into the jackpot? That was another hundred to one chance. Why hadn't it gone down to the box behind, and lain there, safe and hidden, until a month later when they emptied the box, and nobody would be there to see it, or notice it, or remember anything about it? It looked like a conscious chain of animus, trying to get him all tangled up in what he knew was the perfect crime.

He moved his chair back from the table. Janey Blake had it now, and he had to get it. He couldn't afford to take any chances now, not even a hundred-to-one chance, or a thousand-to-one. He'd figured all the chances, prepared for them intelligently and carefully. This was an off-chance he could never have foreseen. And he had to move fast. Not even Janey Blake, not Janey or anybody, was going to stand in his way. He knew more about Janey now. He was prepared to deal with her if he had to. What was Janey or Janey's life even when his own was hanging precariously in the balance?

ELEVEN

WHEN GUS BLAKE got downstairs his breakfast was on the side of
the gas stove keeping warm for him, the percolator in front of his
place set on the red-and-white-checked tablecloth on the counter in
front of the window. Janey and little Jane were through, their dishes
washed and on the drain board to dry. He could see them through the
window in the back yard, Janey in a red sweater, the sleeves pushed
up above her elbows, settling the little Dane in her white picket play
pen with her sandbox, building blocks and doll's house and the narrow
street Janey had constructed among them so she could wheel her dolls
around. She was bundled up in a blue snow suit and white hood and
mittens, rosy-cheeked and laughing in the crisp November morning.
Gus watched her tumble and right herself, and set off to her busy work
at the sandbox. He smiled and poured himself a cup of coffee.

"I'm a hell of a father," he thought. It was supposed to be his job
to get up in the morning while Janey got breakfast and put little Jane
out in her yard so Janey could get on with her own busy work, but it
had been over a month since he'd done it. He'd been sweating over
the Centennial edition half the nights, and now with the Wernitz business on top of all of it he'd be pressed even harder. And it wasn't only
the Wernitz business. He poured another cup of coffee, got his plate
from the stove and sat down at the counter table, his eye still on the
yard.

He was worried about Janey. She wasn't acting like herself at all,
except when she was with the little Dane. She was all right when she
was with her, but not with anybody else. Not with him, certainly. It
had been slowly dawning on him for a week or so. He watched her
catch the rubber ball little Jane threw from the sandbox and toss it
back. She was shaking her head then, shivering, pretending she was
cold, and running back toward the steps, laughing and waving back
at the little Dane. Almost at the brick walk by the side of the house
she stopped abruptly, looking down at the ground. Gus craned his neck
to see what it was. He thought, "Oh, hell." It was a bare damp place
where the water from the downspout at the corner of the house col-

lected, that he'd promised to fix and never got around to. It hadn't
rained for three days. The little Dane wasn't likely to get her feet
muddy or slip on it—not when she was in her pen at least.

Janey was still looking at it. He saw her go over and pull four thin
bamboo stakes out of a clump of chrysanthemums in the side border,
and start back to the bare patch in the grass. She turned then and
looked up at the house, at the upper windows, before she looked at
the kitchen window and saw him. He grinned and waved, but she
didn't smile back. She just stood there a moment, tossed the stakes
over on the border again, brushed her hands lightly together, and came
on toward the back door, looking around casually as she came. Gus
swore a little. He'd get somebody to come and fix the blasted drain-
pipe and patch up the triple-blasted lawn if that was what she was
sore about. Or he'd go do it himself. There was probably grass seed
in the garden box in the basement. This was the one place he'd ever
lived in or worked in where what you needed any given moment was
right there where it was supposed to be.

Now, if Janey could only read and write, she'd be a hell of a lot
more use around the *Gazette* than Connie Maynard or anybody else
he could think of just offhand. He watched her run back and pick up
the little Dane, who'd pitched over with her doll buggy and was yelling
bloody murder one second and laughing her head off the next. He sat
down again and looked at his watch. It was time to be shoving, but
he had to talk to Janey. She'd left the play pen and gone down toward
the end of the yard, just sort of mooning around, he thought irritably;
it wasn't quite the weather to be out looking for crocuses or whatever,
with only a light sweater on. Then suddenly it struck Gus Blake that
she wasn't coming on. Something else struck him at the same time, a
non sequitur in one sense, sequitur as hell in another. It was something
Connie Maynard had said as they'd got to her house when he drove
home with her at two-thirty that morning. He could still hear her saying it.

"Gus—I don't want to louse up any of your illusions, precious, but
hasn't it ever occurred to you that maybe your Janey just a little tiny
bit regrets not marrying Orvie Rogers instead of you? She'd have a
cook and maids and clothes and she wouldn't have to get up and cook
your breakfast and wash your clothes. You're wonderful, of course,
dear, and amusing and terribly intelligent—but it's all on a special level
that Janey must find pretty rotten dull at times . . . if you don't mind

my saying so. After all, she's young and she could easily like to have a
little fun once in a while. But I'm sorry, angel. I shouldn't have said
it. But you are a little self-centered, aren't you? I mean—"

He could hear himself too. "Janey and I get on all right, Connie—
thanks just the same." Stiff like, putting Miss Maynard right back in
her own place. He could hear her laugh as she'd bent over and kissed
him lightly on the cheek.

"Okay, darling. You'll find out. Everybody else knows it. And sometime you're going to want to kiss me good night . . . and will I let
you? I sure will. We're the same sort, Gus. Janey's too sweet for either
of us. We're both stinkers at heart, dear. Well, good night, Gus. Thanks
for bringing me home."

He got up, took his dishes over to the sink and turned on the hot
water. He stood there for a moment, looking down at them. There
was a lot in it. Somehow, he'd realized it all a long time ago; in fact,
when he married Janey. The idea of permanance had not really been
part of it, not that he'd thought about it rationally in any such terms
but because impermanence was something he just naturally took for
granted. You had a job in New York in February and in San Francisco
in March, and in May you were in London helping cover a war that
was knocking everything people had thought was permanent to very
small bits and to hell with it. Connie Maynard had come as near to
the idea of permanence as he'd ever particularly thought of, during
the war and just after it, when permanence in your personal non-ma-
terial life had taken on a peculiar importance. But Connie had cured
him of that quaint idea.

He put his dishes on the drain board with Janey's and little Jane's. It
wasn't until Connie sounded off the night before that he'd thought
much about any of it again. Or after he'd left her, rather, and started
to walk home and decided to go down to the paper and write up the
Wernitz deal instead. It was one of the nice things about a newspaper.
Everything was so damned current. You didn't have time to worry
about the past, or the future—or even your own personal present. He
went into the pantry and stood there, listening, to see if, now he was
out of the window and out of the kitchen, Janey would come on in.
And after a few minutes she did. He heard her shut the door and stop
at the sink, surprised, probably, that he'd cleared and washed his
dishes. Then she came on toward the pantry.

"Oh," she said. She stopped, her eyes wide as they always were, but different, as if she had pulled an opaque blue curtain down behind them. "Oh. I thought you'd probably gone. You must have a lot to do, don't you? I'm going down to Mother's as soon as I get the beds made."

"Janey." As he stepped toward her he trod on the loose board in front of the pantry door. It creaked loudly. Her body tensed and he saw her fists clench tightly. She was nervous as a cat. As he stepped off the board it creaked again. "I'm sorry," he said. "I really will get a carpenter to come fix that." He'd said it dozens of times, but she'd always laughed. She didn't even smile now.

"You've said that before. But it's all right. It doesn't matter."

It made it harder for him to go on, but he did.

"Janey, if I've done anything peculiarly and especially obnoxious to you, I'm sorry," he said seriously. "I'm sorry I was so late last night, and I'm sorry I wasn't up in time to drive your mother home this morning."

He could hear the Court House clock strike nine. Half an hour late now. He was always at his desk by eight-thirty. He saw Janey's eyes move off, listening to it too, and it seemed to him listening for something else. The light flush that stained her cheeks when he mentioned her mother faded. He looked at her intently. "Your mother did stay all night, didn't she?"

She flushed again, and hesitated, moistening her lips. Then she turned her blue eyes up to his. "No. I told a lie," she said warmly. "She went back home as soon as I came in."

He stared at her. "What the—" He stopped himself abruptly. What was the matter with him? He was always getting sore at somebody lately. And Janey was getting sore too. Sore at him. That was something that had never happened before. "I'm sorry," he said.

"It doesn't matter. But I want you to quit saying 'What the hell' to me. Just quit it! I won't stand for it any more. And quit saying you'll have the floor board fixed or the drain pipe fixed, or any of the other things you're always going to do and never think of any more. Because it doesn't matter. I don't want you to do *anything* around here. All I want you to do is go away and go on about your own business, and let me go on about mine!"

She could hear herself saying things she didn't mean and didn't care about, because she was angry and wounded still from last night, and bitterly resentful. But she did mean part of it. She did want him to get out of the house before the police came. She had to get him out before they came. This was her business. She'd started it without him, and waited desperately for him to come and take it out of her hands, and he came and brought Connie Maynard and was cross and rude to her. Connie was rude and offensive—"It's her dining room, isn't it?"— raising her eyebrows, belittling Janey's taste and Janey's pride—and then he'd gone off with Connie and stayed until five o'clock in the morning. And he could go again. He could go back to Connie and leave her to go on taking care of herself and little Jane. She could do it very well. She didn't need any one to stand around and act as if she were a stupid little fool, and get sore at her because she was trying to do her job the best she could.

She tried to listen out the back way and out the front at the same time. She had to have Gus out of the way when the police came. She didn't want him ever to know what had happened the night before. He could go away and stay until five o'clock with Connie. Let him go to her now. She didn't want him there any more. The police would be there soon, to fingerprint the fuse box in the basement. And there was the thing she'd just discovered out in the damp bare patch near the brick walk.

It was a large clear footprint made by some one who was running. The sole of the shoe was quite deep and the heel barely showed at all. It was headed toward the end of the garden. Even if there weren't fingerprints in the basement, a footprint would help. But somehow, during the night, either asleep or awake, she had become convinced of the importance of finding out who had come into the house. It was some one who wanted something. It wasn't the few bits of silver on the sideboard, and she had no jewelry anybody would want. It had to be something else . . . and there was only one thing she had that was of any value. She'd thought it over and over again in the night. That was little Jane.

She caught her breath now and held it for an instant before she turned and ran out into the kitchen. It hadn't occurred to her until that moment that if they'd come into the house to take little Jane they could just as easily come into the yard. . . . But little Jane was there, playing in the sandbox.

"Janey! What is the matter with you?"

As Gus followed her into the kitchen she flashed around at him, her eyes hot, her lips trembling. "Just go, will you? Just go and leave

me alone! That's all that's the matter with me! I just don't want you
to be here—I want to be alone!"

He stood there a moment, a little dazed and unbelieving. This was
incredible. This wasn't Janey at all. It was some one he'd never known
or heard of. It was as if the little Dane's white lop-eared rabbit had
suddenly turned into a snarling wildcat at the foot of the crib. And
as he took a step backward to retire with whatever dignity he could
manage, she turned around and flew out into the yard. He saw her at
the play pen, turned and went back through the pantry. As he stepped
on the creaking board again, a wave of anger flashed up in him.—
Drain pipes, bare spots in the grass, loose boards. By God, he'd fix
one of them anyway. He opened the basement door, banged it shut
behind him and went downstairs. The garden box was in the corner
by the area door. He yanked it open. Lime, fertilizer, grass seed. He
picked up the seed and took the rake off the hook behind the box.
He could hear Janey upstairs in the kitchen, and he waited until he
heard her go through the pantry and dining room and start upstairs
with little Jane. He opened the area door and went up to the ground
level. A colored boy with a bamboo leaf rake was coming around the
side of the house.

"You want the leaves raked up?"

"Yeah," Gus said. "Here. Take this." He handed him the box of grass
seed. "See that patch there? Rake it up and seed it. If you know anybody that can fix a drain spout, tell 'em to come and fix it and send
me the bill."

He went back down the area steps into the basement, hung up his
rake, closed the garden box and went upstairs. The hinge on the door
whined as he closed and latched it. The loose board creaked as he
went into the dining room. He took his overcoat and hat off the chair
and started out. At the front door he turned. Maybe there was still
something he could say to Janey. He looked up the stair well. She
was standing up there, holding to the rail, looking down, her face
frozen into the most extraordinary mask.

"Janey—for God's sake, what—"

She drew her body erect and taut. "Oh," she said. "It's you. I . . . I
thought you'd gone. Please . . . please go." She turned away slowly
and disappeared toward little Jane's room.

For a moment Gus stood there, not knowing what to do. He took
off his coat and put it and his hat on the chair. He couldn't leave her

like this. As he turned to go up the stairs, he heard some one come
onto the porch and heard the doorbell ring through the dining room
from the pantry. And heard Janey's footsteps on the top floor, running
out into the hall. He went to the door and opened it. He said, "Oh.
Oh, hello, Orvie."

Orvie Rogers' mouth dropped open a little. "Oh," he said. "I . . .
I thought you'd gone to the office. I . . . I just stopped by to speak
to Janey."

For a moment Gus stood there motionless. It was only a moment,
but it seemed to him a very long time indeed before he could unloosen
his hand from the door knob and get his vocal cords in a fit order to
function sensibly and audibly. It evidently seemed a long time to Orvie
Rogers. He swallowed before he said, "It . . . it wasn't important
anyway, Gus. I . . . I'll come back later. It was just something—"

"Not at all," Gus said. He could hear the false cheery cordiality
in his voice and knew he was sounding like a third-rate aristocrat in
a bad movie. "Not at all," he said again. "Come in. I was just leaving." He got the door knob out of his hand, got back into the hall and
picked up his hat and coat again. "I was just shoving off."

He managed to move toward the stairs. She was up there, looking
expectantly over the banister rail, one hand up, breathlessly holding on
to the neck of her red sweater. He caught the briefest glimpse of her,
not having meant to look up, not wanting to see her caught out. "Oh,
God!" he thought; "not Janey!" The saliva that flushed into his mouth
was bitter as wormwood and gall. He swallowed it down with an effort
that wrenched and churned the food in his stomach, tasting it sour and
bilious again. No wonder she was so damned anxious to get him out
of the house. He controlled himself deliberately, sick at himself for
being able to make his voice sound as if everything was swell. Everything perfectly fine.

"It's Orvie, Janey."

"—*Orvie?*" He could see her swallow and moisten her lips. "What
. . . what does he want, Gus?"

He was rather proud of himself then. In a way. He sounded fine as
he said, "I don't know. Why don't you come on down and ask him?
I've got to shove off. So long." He started to the door. "Or why don't
you go on up to the living room, Orvie? I'll see you later."

"Okay," Orvie Rogers said.

Gus closed the front door and went down the walk. Or he assumed he did. He found himself at his desk a little while later. At least he guessed it was his desk. Swede Carlson was sitting beside it waiting for him, talking to Connie Maynard while he waited.

TWELVE

"MORNING, GUS." Connie Maynard's cheerful lilt gave his stomach another wrench. She made it sound as if they'd just had breakfast together but don't ever let anybody else know our beautiful, lovely secret. One colorless eye of Swede Carlson flickered. Gus felt the other cocked bleakly on him as he hung his overcoat on the hook by the washbowl in the corner and stuck his hat on top of it. The hell with both of them. He turned back. Swede Carlson looked at him disinterestedly.

"Thought you came back and did your story last night," he said.

"That's right," Gus answered curtly. "Got anything to add to it? I thought you were going home and go to bed."

"Oh, oh," Connie Maynard thought. "He's mad about something. I bet little sheep-eyes gave him one hell of a going over this morning."

She had a bright picture of Janey trailing lugubriously around in her old yellow bathrobe and wool-lined slippers, no lipstick, tow hair unkempt, red-nosed, probably weeping into his coffee cup. She caught a quick glimpse of herself, crisply tailored and neat, in the cracked mirror over the washbowl, and smiled at it before she moved around and perched on the corner of his desk, looking casual but businesslike, waiting for orders. Chief Carlson was cutting something off an oblong brown block. She shuddered inside a little. She hadn't known people still chewed tobacco.

"I did go home, just like I said," Carlson said placidly. He closed his knife and put it and the plug back in his pocket. "But I got up this morning. Still haven't got anythin' to add, not right now. The boy's still out, over at the hospital." He put on his hat. "I'm just makin' a few calls. Routine check-up, I guess you people call it."

His bleak gaze was still fixed on Gus. If it meant anything, Gus Blake, embroiled in his own special kettle of bitterly simmering oil, was missing it. He jerked his chair up to the desk.

"Then why don't you get on and make 'em," he said offensively.

"Tell me about it later. But just get the hell out of here, will you? You, too, Connie. Both of you. Clear out and shut the door. Cut out all the yakkety-yak, for just five minutes. I've got to work."

"Thought maybe I'd like to see that editorial I hear you wrote," Carlson said equably. "Understand you—"

"Okay, okay. I'm not pulling it, if that's what you want to know. I'm letting it ride just like it is. Connie'll get it for you. Now get out, will you? Get out before I throw you out."

He heard the door close as they went into Connie Maynard's small office next to his, and waited a moment before he stretched his head up and back as far as he could, gritting his teeth, staring up at the stains on the grimy ceiling. He was sick as a horse. If there was only some place he could go and get the hell out of here. Get drunk, he thought; go out and get lousy stinking drunk and just forget about the whole business. He jerked his head forward again and pushed his chair violently back, got up, started toward his overcoat in the corner, stopped and came slowly back. He was drunk already—or his stomach felt as if he had been drunk. It was churning now; it had the classic dimensions of a first-class hangover. Anyway, getting polluted and going through it all over again wasn't going to help. It never had and it never would.

He ripped his handkerchief out and blew his nose. In a minute or two he was going to bawl like the little Dane. It was going to be the second time in his life he'd wanted to cry, the first time since he'd been in the hospital plane flying in to Pearl from Iwo Jima and bawling didn't help any more than getting boiled did. He blew his nose again, and sat down in his chair. *Forget it, Blake. Just take it*—socko, wham—take it and shut up.

He stuck a sheet of paper in his typewriter and stared at it until it gradually came into focus and the room gathered itself together, everything coming back into solid form and settling itself firmly where he was used to seeing it. It settled back, but it was all changed. All small time, all down at the heel. A rattling typewriter on a rattle-trap desk in the back room of a run-down building that ought to have been condemned before the Civil War. . . . What the hell was he doing there? What the hell was he doing sitting in a room with "Managing Editor" printed on the door . . . the G and E rubbed off so that it read "Managin ditor"? What was he doing there anyway? Grubbing away at a hundred bucks a week on the understanding that if he pulled the paper out of the red in four years he could buy a controlling interest in it over the next four years at the appraised value the day he came to it. . . . It was all funny as hell, now he was seeing it with the fish scales off his eyes. Whatever—? But that brought him to Janey again, and he wasn't going to think about Janey. That had been his first mistake. Blake. Blake, the lion in the street, doing a favor because he had a little time to spare.

A copy boy kicking the door brought him to sharply. "Come in!" he bellowed. "And next time knock! Don't kick the damn door down, you little—" He swung around, hearing himself and seeing the astonished boy. "Sorry," he said quickly. "Sorry. I take it all back. Just put it in the basket, will you, Ty."

"—Here it is." Connie Maynard pulled the proof sheet of the day's editorial off the holder by her desk and glanced at it again. It was how she knew Gus must have come back to the office to work after he'd left her at her door a little before three o'clock. The first few lines under the head "Suckers" had been changed.

Slot machine operators come and go. They go quietly sometimes. Sometimes they're murdered before they get a chance to go quietly. Like Doc Wernitz out at Newton's Corner last night.
The suckers who play them go on forever.

The rest of it was the same. She handed it over to Swede Carlson.

"You know, Chief," she said, sitting down at her desk, "I don't think Gus has the faintest idea that his wife is in such a mess over the slot machines."

She pulled her chair up abruptly to cover her own surprise.—Was that why he was so all-fired mad? It hadn't occurred to her until that second. That was the trouble with the egotistic approach. She could almost hear her father saying it to her. She had simply taken for granted that the row between Gus and Janey must have been over her. And row there had been—she knew Gus too well to make any mistake about that—but what she'd just thought of was much more likely. She looked at Carlson. He had his horn-rimmed reading glasses on, concentrated on the editorial. She pulled forward a bunch of rewrite stuff the boy had put on her desk while she was talking to him in Gus's office, and glanced at the top sheet. It was the report from the blotter at the City Police Station for the twenty-four preceding hours, and never very interesting. Today there was a scribbled note clipped to it. She picked it up and read it.

"Con.—Guess Blake will want to write up his own four-alarm burglary." The reporter's initials were penciled at the bottom.

She read it again, and read the story as it had been written leaving the Blakes' four-alarm burglary out. Then she looked over at Chief Carlson to ask him, and changed her mind. He was County Police anyway, and this was something that needed a little time to think about. She put the story back on her desk face down and took a cigarette out of the box in front of her. Carlson was just about to the end of the editorial now, and he'd be gone in a minute.

He put the proof sheets down on the desk. "So Mrs. Blake is in a mess with the slot machines, is she?" he asked soberly. "Why do you say that, Miss Maynard?"

Connie was too surprised to think of anything at all to say for an instant. "Oh," she said. "Why, I . . . I supposed you knew it. Everybody in town seems to—except Gus. I'm really sorry. I wouldn't have peeped, but I thought that was the reason you were giving Gus such a fish-eyed stare in there. Let's just skip it, shall we? It would make it frightfully awkward for me."

A bleak smile lighted Carlson's heavy face a little. "You mean you think maybe, because Mrs. Blake's lost a couple of hundred—"

He stopped. "More than a couple of hundred, is it?"

"I must be horribly transparent, Chief." Connie laughed. "But you're right. It is rather more than that."

"A lot of people are more transparent than they think, Miss Maynard," Carlson said. "But say she was in the hole a couple of thousand even, you won't think I think Gus Blake went out there and slugged Doc Wernitz on that account, now, will you, Miss Maynard? Maybe I'm dumber 'n I think I am, but I'm not that dumb. There's another thing maybe you *could* tell me. About this deal Gus has got with your father. About the paper, I mean."

Connie looked at him a moment. She said, "Thanks for telling me something. I supposed they had some kind of . . . deal. I don't know what it is. Perhaps you'd better ask my father. Or Gus. What's that got to do with Mr. Wernitz getting murdered?"

Swede Carlson shook his head. "Nothin', Miss Maynard. Nothin' in particular. I just wondered, that's all. I'm interested in a lot of things, right now. What Wernitz did with all the dough he made, for instance. Whether he left a will. What made him decide to get out of town. Who he talked to about it. Who'd profit by havin' him dead. A lot of things like that, Miss Maynard."

He took his hat off the corner of her desk. "I guess you're pretty new on this murder business," he said. "You were pretty upset, last night, it looked like to me."

He's watching me. I'm transparent. She kept her eyes wide and interested, not blank, fixed on his face.

"I'm very new to it. It did upset me."

"That's what I figured." Swede Carlson nodded his understanding.

"Well, I'll tell you, Miss Maynard. I've been Chief here in Smith County for fifteen years next April. I've seen a lot of people killed, one way and another. When men kill each other, it's when they get juiced up and blood mad. It's quick, then—quick and easy for the cops, too. Or a little fella can get scared of a big fella and not see any other road out. Or jealousy. Sometimes one fella thinks another one's hangin' around his wife too much."

He shrugged his heavy shoulders as if that was just one of those things nobody could ever do anything about.

"But by and large, Miss Maynard, when one fella sets out and does a neat premeditated killin', it's because the other fella could put him in jail for swindlin' him out of somethin'—money, property, somethin' the fella stole from him . . . and the funny thing, it's not so much him keepin' the money, or the property, of the fella he stole it from as it is him keepin' his own reputation. You know, Miss Maynard, I figure most killin's that are premeditated, like the one we've got here, come because people are just plain cowards."

The bleak eyes rested steadily on her.

"If you're rich you're afraid to lose your money *and* your reputation. But if you had to take your choice, it's always your reputation. That's the most important, just the same as if you were poor. I guess reputation's mighty important, no matter how you look at it."

Chief Carlson went over to the door. "Well, I guess I got to go. I better be thinkin' about my own reputation. If I don't get this business cleared up, I'll be out on a rotten limb for fair.—Ain't often I get a chance to talk to a real intelligent lady." He opened the door. "Tell Gus I'll be back. I'd give him time to cool down a little first, if I was you."

Constance Maynard sat motionless in her chair for several moments.

Keeping her face rigidly as it was she pulled open her desk drawer and reached for the mirror under the pile of papers in it. She held it up in front of her. Transparent. He'd said people were more transparent than they knew . . . but she'd known while he was still sitting there how transparent she'd become. The mirror only proved what her dry slightly parted lips and the strained feeling along her eyelids had already told her. The rouge stood out in queer patches on her cheeks. She moistened her lips, blinked her eyes and put the mirror in the drawer again.

He was talking about her father, of course. All the time he'd been pretending to talk about his experience with murder, he'd really been talking about John Maynard. She tried to think when it was she'd first become aware of it, but everything he'd said was so mixed up in her mind that she couldn't think back over it and say when it was she knew that was what he was telling her. She got up and paced back and forth in the little room. Her father . . . Her father who'd told her at breakfast that it was best to keep her little nose out of things that were none of her business. She flung herself into the armchair again. But that was absurd. Her father had been at home. He was out in the pantry seeing about the liquor for the party when she got there at half-past five. When was Wernitz killed? She caught the proof off the rack and ran her eye quickly down Gus's story. Between 5:45 and 7:00. The service mechanic had phoned the police at 12 minutes to 10:00. According to the story, he had told them when they got out there and found him down in the basement with Wernitz's body that he had come back from a call at 6:35 approximately, and found Wernitz dead, after he had tried to turn on the lights in the office and gone down to fix the fuse.

Five-forty-five and seven. Connie put the proof sheet down. At five-thirty her father was in the service pantry. At a quarter to seven he was in the library, dressed for dinner, talking to her about Janey's checks. It was impossible for him to have got out to Newton's Corner, killed Wernitz and—. She stopped and clenched her jaws, her cheeks flaming hot all of a sudden. How dared she even consider anything so stupid and revolting. . . . It was like blasphemy even to think of it. Swede Carlson had better watch out who he was talking about.

She gave her head a violent shake and looked at her watch. As soon as she got through the stuff in front of her, she'd call her father up and ask him to meet her at the Sailing Club for lunch. *Never.* Never in all her life had she heard anything so foul and revolting, underhanded and positively rotten. She picked up the sheet with the police reports on it and the note attached. The next thing, they'd be saying John Maynard had burgled the Blake house. . . . She got up, went over to the door to Gus's office and wrenched it open.

"Smitty says do you want to write the—"

She had got that much of it out before she saw Gus was not at his desk. A sheet of blank paper was sticking out of his typewriter—blank, but in too crooked for anybody to write on it. She glanced over at the corner by the wash basin. His hat and coat were gone.

"Where in the world—"

She turned quickly as the *Gazette's* crime reporter, who also covered the financial district, consisting of the three banks on Court House Square, and the industrial district, which was the Rogers plant across Carson Creek, came in the door.

"What do I do about the Blakes' burglar?" he inquired testily. "They're going over to fingerprint the joint. Do I cover it or does—"

"I don't know. If he'd wanted it in, I guess he'd have said so. He didn't, so I guess he doesn't. Anyway, he's gone. I don't know where he is. Where's his secretary? Ask her, don't ask me."

"She's home sick with a cold in the head."

"Then skip it," Connie Maynard snapped. "He's probably gone home himself if the police are there."

"Keep your shirt on." He started to close the door. "It's okay with me. I don't know what's the matter with everybody this morning."

"Wait, Smitty." She came out of a red fog and started functioning again. "What is this four-alarm burglary? What happened?"

"Oh, nothing much," Smitty said indifferently. "Just a guy in the house and Mrs. Blake scared him out. I just figured maybe there was an angle. The guy switched the lights out in the basement, like the Wernitz deal. But I guess Blake got that as easy as I did. I thought of telling Swede Carlson, but he was in there, so I guess Gus already told him. I've got to do the market report now. You can get winter kale for fifteen cents a bunch at Tony Modesto's when you put your two bucks down on Crater's Fancy—he's a cinch for the three o'clock at Bowie."

THIRTEEN

CONNIE waited until the door shut, closing out the roar of the presses. Her teeth bit down over her full lower lip. So that was it; that was why Janey was downstairs at half-past two in the morning. But why hadn't Gus said anything about it to Carlson? Why was he keeping it out of the paper? She lighted another cigarette, went over to the soot-stained window and looked down through the coarse screen grating at the garbage cans in the area that belonged to the lunch room next door, without being conscious of them for the first time in six months. Unless . . . Was it possible Gus didn't know anything about it? She shrugged the idea off at once. Janey would hardly miss the chance to be a heroine. Some things didn't make sense. In fact, she thought suddenly, nothing made sense. She saw the garbage cans then and smelled the stale grease and dishwater seeping in around the window pane, or imagined she did, and went back to her desk. If she got the paper out by herself today, she'd have a talking point with her father. She sat down and got to work, laughing suddenly. The idea of getting him to give her the paper to save himself income tax must have been developing quietly in her subconscious mind all night. She remembered how it had occurred to her at the party while she was waiting for Gus to come. She'd settled for Gus, then. Today she rather thought she'd have them both.

She wheeled her typewriter around and set to work feeding out her own copy until she came across a précis Gus had written for a box on the front page. It was headed with a large question mark. Under it was: "Who Murdered Doc Wernitz?"

She read it intently.

The following are the known facts about Paul M. Wernitz.

He was 61 years old.
He was born in Czecho-Slovakia.
He came to the United States in 1909 at the age of 20.
He was naturalized in Tacoma, Washington, in 1919.
He went to Carson City, Nevada, in 1921 and worked there in a gambling establishment, buying a controlling interest in it in 1926.

He came to Smith County in 1931, organized the Smith County Recreation Company Incorporated in 1936.

He bought the Chapman farm at Newton's Corner in 1935.

He lived alone in the main farmhouse.

At the time of his murder last night, the former kitchen wing of the farmhouse was being occupied by Ralph (Buzz) Rodriguez, Wernitz's assistant and service mechanic.

He employed five other assistants.

He kept the lights on in the house from sundown to sunup from a pathological fear of the dark.

He employed no household help.

He is reputed to have been a wealthy man.

He was known, though not generally, to be closing his house and leaving Smith County.

Those are the known facts about Doc Wernitz. These are the known facts surrounding his murder as this paper got them from the Chief of the Smith County Constabulary, Henry L. (Swede) Carlson.

Doc Wernitz was expected to return to Newton's Corner yesterday at 5:30 P.M.

At 5:15 P.M., Buzz Rodriguez turned the lights on in the main house, except for the old farmhouse parlor, which Wernitz used as his office and kept locked.

Buzz Rodriguez, George Jeffers, Franklin Thomas and James Mason, service mechanics, were in the downstairs office of the kitchen wing at 5:00 P.M. waiting as usual to go on service calls.

Buzz Rodriguez's story, as coherently as the police are able to make it out, is as follows:

He was not on duty until 8:00 P.M. but he was there at the house because a girl he expected to see had to work all day. Three calls for service came between 5:00 and 5:20. They were from widely separated parts of the county. A fourth call came at 5:24 from Heron Point. Buzz Rodriguez left a note under Wernitz's door and took the call. He returned to the house at 6:20. The lights were not on in Wernitz's office. He went in the house and saw the office door open. He tried the lights, found them out of order and went down in the basement to replace the fuse. There he either fell or was struck on the head.

He is now in the General Hospital with severe concussion, under police guard until Chief Carlson can talk to him.

The three other service mechanics returned from their calls some time after eight o'clock. Those calls were false alarms. The proprietors of the establishments denied they put such calls through. Four other calls were made after eight o'clock.

Buzz Rodriguez called the police at 10.02 P.M. and reported Wernitz's murder.

The police say he sounded excited and incoherent.

They arrived at the house at 10:09 and found Buzz Rodriguez in the cellar with Wernitz's body.

The fuse controlling the lights in Wernitz's office had been unscrewed and was lying on the cellar floor.

The iron bar the murderer used to crush Wernitz's skull was lying bloodstained beside him.

Buzz Rodriguez collapsed and was found injured, by Chief Carlson, at 12:42 while awaiting questioning under technical arrest.

Who killed Doc Wernitz? The *Smithville Gazette* will pay a reward of $1000 for information leading to the arrest and conviction of Doc Wernitz's murderer.

Connie Maynard read it through, turned back to the first half and read it through again. She sat looking down at it. Gus didn't know anything about Doc Wernitz. He'd told her so on the way out to Newton's Corner. Nobody knew anything about him. Her father had told her that. He hadn't known Wernitz was a Czech, when he'd come to America, or anything about him at all. She was still wondering about it, slightly dazed, when her door opened.

"Hi, Connie. How about some lunch?"

She looked up, startled. "Oh, hello, Dorsey. How are you? I'd love it. Is it lunch time?"

She looked at her watch, surprised, and then glanced through the door into Gus's office. He still wasn't back. She was still in a semi-bewildered fog. How and where had Gus got so much dope about Wernitz—and when? That was even more amazing.

"I wish banking was that fascinating," Dorsey Syms said, grinning at her. "Or maybe it's the food at our house. I always know damned well when it's pushing twelve."

"I usually do too." Connie laughed. "But this really is fascinating. Look at it. Did you know this or any of it about Doc Wernitz?"

Dorsey propped himself on the edge of her desk and took the proof. "All I knew about him was he was a handsome customer at the Smithville Trust Company," he said. "Carlson was in this morning. Boy, do I wish I had the dough that old buzzard Wernitz had." He read the two columns of the box, and shook his head. "I didn't know any of this, except the Newton's Corner end of it. I always understood nobody knew where he came from. Or anything about him, till he got here." He tossed the sheet back on the desk. "Lunch?"

"Oh . . ." Connie remembered abruptly. "I was going to call Dad and ask him to take me down to the Sailing Club." Her yellow-green eyes smouldered as she thought of what Chief Carlson had really been saying to her.

Dorsey Syms grinned and shook his head. "He can't afford it, Connie. Not today he can't."

"What do you mean?"

She controlled herself sharply. She hadn't meant to sound alarmed, but she did.

"Hey, I didn't mean it! All I meant was that he's through being generous for the day." He laughed and got Connie's coat off the hanger behind the door. "I didn't know he was that fond of our Janey."

Connie pushed her chair back. "Will you tell me what you're talking about?"

"It's hush stuff, Con. Confidential as hell. He covered Janey's overdraft for her this morning. Three hundred and twenty bucks' worth of nice new overdraft. You should have seen Fergie. He almost had tears in his eyes, his secretary told me."

He helped her on with her coat.

"I think it's swell. I just wonder why he did it, is all."

"Why shouldn't he?" She took her compact out of her bag and powdered her nose. *Why on earth had he done that? What had happened? What earthly reason . . .*

"Well, don't snap at me, Con," Dorsey said equably. "It's none of my business. All I was wondering was what Carlson's going to think. Your father isn't a noted philanthropist. Or didn't you know that? Or am I wrong? Anyway, it's a bank secret. I guess I shouldn't have told you. For Pete's sake don't tell him I told you. I've got trouble enough on my hands as it is."

"Why? What trouble have you got?" Not that she cared. She had trouble of her own she'd rather worry about just now.

"That's why I'm taking you to lunch, baby. *I* need an alibi!"

He grinned at her as she looked at him blankly. "You . . . you need an alibi?"

"That's what I said. Come on to lunch and I'll explain it."

Her pulse quickened as she snapped her bag shut and took her gloves out of her pocket.

"Fine," she said. "Come on."

If Dorsey Syms needed an alibi, she was thinking quickly, she'd be glad to help him. If her father needed one, then Dorsey's could crash. The minute the police knew . . . There were people Connie would rather have thrown to the wolves. Dorsey Syms was the only one begging for it. She smiled brightly at him as they went through the press rooms.

She stopped just before they got to the door to wave over to the dry old man in his shirt sleeves at the desk marked "City Editor," in the corner by the front window. "Good-by, Ed, I'm going out to lunch." Dorsey opened the long plate-glass door into the narrow vestibule. He stood aside, holding it open for some one coming in the storm door from the street.

"Cheese it, the cops!" He grinned back at Connie, and at the tall thin man who had stopped and was holding the storm door open for them to come on through. "Raiding the joint, Bill? You know my cousin Constance Maynard? This is Lieutenant Williams, Connie."

"Oh," Connie said. The smile faded from her eyes. "Of course." She recognized him now he'd taken off his green felt hat. "How are you? Is there anything I can do for you before I go out? Gus Blake isn't here."

Lieutenant Williams stepped back into the street.

"No, it was Gus I wanted to see," he said. "I've just been down to his place. About that entry he had last night. Where is he, do you know? I'd like to get in touch with him."

"I don't know where he is," Connie said.

She looked over at the empty space along the Reserved line in front of the *Gazette* building. "His car's gone. Maybe he's gone with Chief Carlson out to the Wernitz house. But I don't know, Lieutenant. He came in this morning and left right away. I assumed he'd gone home."

—And if he hadn't, she was thinking, maybe he really didn't know about the entry, as Williams called it. Even Gus wouldn't be that casual about his possessions—she hoped. She turned to her cousin.

"You haven't seen him?"

"Not since he was in the bank. That was about ten-thirty. I didn't get a chance to talk to him."

The detective put his hat back on. "It's funny he wouldn't stick around," he said. "Around home, I mean." He seemed more puzzled than perturbed. "You were with him, I understand, Miss Maynard. When he got home last night. Didn't he seem to think there might be some connection between the entry and the Wernitz deal? I just told Swede Carlson. He hadn't heard about it. That's the trouble with this County-City set-up. Your right hand don't know anything about your left one till the trail's stone cold. What did Gus say about it, Miss Maynard?"

"He didn't say a thing," Connie said. "Nothing at all. I don't think he knew anything about it. Mrs. Blake didn't mention it while I was there. And Gus certainly wouldn't have gone off and left her and the kid and taken me home if he'd known anything about it."

Lieutenant Williams looked at her.

"Yeah," he said slowly. "Carlson and I both thought it looked a little sort of . . . well, sort of . . ."

He let it hang there without saying sort of what, perhaps because he saw the large figure of the County Chief coming up the street towards the *Gazette* office.

"Well, if you see him tell him Swede and I are looking for him, will you?"

He tipped his hat perfunctorily and walked off to meet Carlson.

Dorsey glanced at his cousin. Her cheeks were flushed a little. She went quickly across the sidewalk to her car and opened the door before he could reach it.

"Why don't you lay off Janey, Con?" he inquired calmly as he stepped in after her and pulled the door shut.

"Why don't you mind your own business, Dorsey?"

She jammed her foot down on the starter. The engine roared. Dorsey saw Carlson and Williams look around at them, and go on talking again. Swede Carlson, his shoulder propped against the telephone pole on the curb, his overcoat open, both hands in his trousers pockets, leaned his head to one side and spat magnificently into the gutter. Dorsey saw that Connie was too annoyed to see that the Chief of the County Police was still looking at the shining green convertible, if Lieutenant Williams was not.

"I'd like to know just where the hell Gus *has* gone," she snapped as she pulled out and into the stream of market-day traffic. "And another thing I'd like to know is just where he got all that inside dope on Wernitz. And what he went to the bank for. He never goes to the bank."

Dorsey Syms reached in his pocket and got out a cigarette. He reached forward and pressed in the lighter on the dash.

"So *I* ought to mind my own business," he remarked equably.

FOURTEEN

JANEY put the last of little Jane's things in the blue canvas suitcase and snapped the lid shut. She hurried, listening breathlessly down the stair well, starting at every rattle and shiver of the house as a truck jolted by in the street, and the creeping sounds in the hot-water pipes up the wall.

"Put Flopsie in too, Mummy." Little Jane came over with the white lop-eared rabbit in her arms. Janey started to refuse, and remembered. She mustn't let little Jane see she was frightened and nervous.

"Of course," she said. "We wouldn't leave Flopsie. Who'd give Flopsie her lunch?"

"And Daddy. Who'll give Daddy his lunch, Mummy?"

Janey's throat tightened. "Daddy'll get his lunch downtown. And we've got to hurry, sweetie. What else shall we take?" She tried not to look down at the troubled blue eyes in the round sober little face turned up to her. "Daddy loves to eat downtown. Hurry, now. We'll take your coat and leggings downstairs and put them on down there, and then we'll get a taxi and go see Grandma. I'll take the suitcase down and you stay here till I come. Here's your book. Look at the pictures till I come back."

She took the suitcase out into the hall. Her own was already packed and waiting at the foot of her bed. She listened a moment, went along to the front room, picked up her hat and coat and looked hastily around. She didn't want to leave anything behind that she'd need and have to come back for, and she had to hurry. She had to get little Jane out of the house. Lieutenant Williams had been there, with his camera and fingerprint powder, soberly going all over the basement and the pantry and dining room, and all over the back yard. The footprint was gone. She hadn't even mentioned it to him. The colored boy was already frightened at the way she'd run out when she saw him seeding the grass where it had been; there was no use for the police to start blaming him. The way they'd moved around and talked when they thought she wasn't listening had destroyed the last poignant hope that somehow none of it had really happened, or that, if it had, it was all over now and there was nothing to worry about any more. But even if it hadn't, she had to get out anyway. The sickening terror in her stomach when she'd heard the basement hinge whine and the pantry board creak was almost more than she could bear, even when she found it was only Gus. He must have thought she was crazy, if he thought about it at all. Or that she was just stupider than usual. If he hadn't thought already she was being stupidly contrary, he'd never have made the fuss about the grass patch and the floor board. And she'd never really cared about either of them. It had always been a joke before.

She looked over the top of her dressing table, pulled open the drawer and saw her evening bag there. The sleeping pills . . . She remembered suddenly. The orange capsules she'd taken from Mrs. Maynard's table. They were still there. The one she'd dropped and Connie had given back to her was halfway to the river by now, or wherever Smithville's sewage went. She took the yellow tissue with the rest of them in it, went to the bathroom and flushed them down to follow it. That really would have been a crazy and stupid thing to do. Who would have taken care of little Jane? It was more than stupid, it was wrong. But it was all over now and somehow very remote, as if it had been another Janey in another life, too hurt and confused to know what she was doing.

She started back to the bedroom and stopped, catching her breath sharply. It was the doorbell. Some one at the front door. Normally she would have run downstairs to open it . . . but nothing was normal in that house any more. "Be careful," Lieutenant Williams had told her. "I don't want to worry you, Mrs. Blake, but you ought to be careful who you let in the house." He hadn't said, "Even if it's somebody you know," but she'd sensed it. Or was it just something inside of herself that told her that? Or just nerves? The bell rang again. She ran to the front room, pushed the window up and looked out.

"Who is it?"

As she saw who it was, her hands tightened on the sill. It was Chief Carlson. The big Swede. Her mouth went dry suddenly. The checks at Wernitz's . . . She realized oddly that she'd forgotten all about that. Even when Orvie Rogers had given her the envelope from his father and mumbled something about slot machines it had seemed all very unreal. There was no time to think about it, then, because the police came right away and Orvie just stuck it in her hand and got out. He probably thought the police would think it was funny, his being there when he should be at the plant. The envelope was in her red sweater pocket in the suitcase now.

But looking out now on Swede Carlson's thick, foreshortened figure, Janey remembered the slot machines again.

"I'll be right down," she called.

She picked up her hat and coat and the suitcases and stopped at little Jane's door. "You read quietly, sweetie, until I get back. I won't be long."

In the front hall she put the suitcase down by the stairs and laid her hat and coat on the chair. She opened the door. "Come in, Mr. Carlson."

He dwarfed the tiny hallway as he came in. It looked even smaller than it did with Gus in it, as tall but not as wide either way. Chief Carlson's eye went straight to the suitcase.

"Goin' somewhere, Mrs. Blake?" he asked pleasantly.

Janey swallowed quickly. Would he think she was trying to run away . . . or try to stop her going?

"Just down to my mother's on Charter Street," she said breathlessly. "I'm taking my litle girl. I've got to go, Mr. Carlson. I . . . I'm afraid to stay here. I—"

"That's a smart idea, Mrs. Blake. I'm glad you're goin'."

So this was Gus Blake's Janey he was always hearing about. She'd been pointed out to him on the street, but he'd never seen her close up without a hat on. Scrawny little thing, compared with Mrs. Carlson anyway. Pretty eyes; washed out—she was scared—but still pretty. What was she scared of him for? Or what else would it be?

"I was just talkin' to Lieutenant Williams," he said. "He told me about you last night. Mighty plucky, Mrs. Blake. I bet Gus was mighty proud of you."

"Gus . . . doesn't know anything about it." She moved back into the dining room. "Would you like to sit down here? The living room's upstairs."

"And your bedroom's on the third floor, I understand. That's where you called the operator from?"

Janey nodded.

"Why didn't you tell Gus, Mrs. Blake?"

As her chin lifted he thought for an instant she was going to say it was none of his business. She turned her blank blue eyes to look not at him but through him. Not as scared now as she was when he came. He waited, wondering if she was going to say "Because Gus came in with Connie Maynard and went out with her and so the hell with Gus, Mr. Carlson."

"He . . . he's very busy," she said. "I didn't think it was important enough to worry him about it."

His bleak eyes rested on her for a moment. "Suppose you show me around, Mrs. Blake," he said quietly. "And tell me all about it." He smiled a little. "I'll be careful not to make any more noise 'n I can help."

He saw the flush creep along Janey's high pale cheek bones. "I'm sorry," he said. He hadn't meant to hurt her feelings.

"It's all right," she said quickly. "I suppose it was stupid of me. But I'm pretty stupid anyway, I guess. But it's just that I . . . I don't want little Jane to grow up always scared of everything, like thunder and the dark and dogs and caterpillars and things. I don't think people have any fun if they're always afraid of everything."

Swede Carlson nodded. "You're right, Mrs. Blake. Doc Wernitz, for instance—he was afraid of the dark. I guess the fella that murdered him—if he should just happen to be the one came here—figured a little slip like you would be too afraid to open her mouth and scream—much less have the pluck and brains to get to the phone right away. I sorta figure that's why he turned the lights off first. So you'd be so scared you wouldn't know what it was he was after."

She was almost to the pantry door on her way to take him down to the basement. She flashed around and stood rigid, her finger tips on the end of the table to steady herself, her eyes wide, changed from blue to sooty black, staring at him, her lips parted, moving soundlessly, repeating the word he had used deliberately.

"—Murdered . . ." He could see her lips frame it.

"I'm afraid so, Mrs. Blake. That's why I'm askin' you to show me around, and tell me everythin' you can think of. Forget all this stuff about your bein' stupid. Gus wouldn't ever have fallen in love with a stupid girl no matter how pretty she was."

He saw he could have saved his breath. She hadn't heard him.

"Oh . . . then you . . . you don't think it's my baby he was after? It's not little Jane?" she gasped. "Oh, if I was sure it wasn't little Jane they were after, I . . . I wouldn't be half as scared!"

The big man's bleak eyes were warmer.

"Because . . . oh, you see we haven't got anything a burglar would want. This silver—" She threw her hand out at the tea service on the sideboard, a wedding present from Orvie Rogers' parents. "That's all we've got that's valuable. And he . . . he went right past it. I couldn't think of anything else they'd want but little Jane—maybe on account of something Gus wrote in the paper. But if it's not little Jane, I'm not afraid any more!"

Swede Carlson mentally shook his head. "The poor kid," he thought. That was why she'd looked out the window upstairs, as though the devil himself might be at the door. His face was a shade grimmer. What a night she must have spent, with Gus off gallivanting all over the country with the Maynard witch. Sometimes it looked like the brighter a fellow was the bigger fool he was. And if Janey Blake was stupid, he'd take them stupid every time. And she really meant it. A little color had come back into her cheeks and her eyes had lost the washed-out stare and come alive again. Afraid of kidnaping . . . not afraid of murder.

"That the way I figure it, Mrs. Blake," he said quietly. "I don't know what he was after. But I don't figure it was any kidnapin'. Now, suppose you just tell me what happened. Everythin', hear?"

The loose board, the whining hinge, the fuse box, clean as a whistle under the gray powder Williams had left, the basement steps, the hinge whining again, the latch clicking, the glow moving slowly and steadily up the stairs . . . Janey heard and saw and explained it all.

"And out here," she said. She opened the kitchen door. "I didn't tell Mr. Williams, because it was gone. It was a man's footprint in the damp ground here, where it washes from the drain spout when it rains. I . . . I'm sorry, but it got raked over this morning. He . . . he must have been running, because the toe was a lot deeper than the heel. It was about an eleven, and sort of pointed. I mean not blunt like your shoes, but sort of narrower at the tip, like an evening ——— "

She stopped, looking up at him, blinking her eyes. Swede Carlson looked down at her. He was reflecting philosophically that if he ever died of apoplexy it wouldn't be in his own bed like a decent God-fearing citizen. It would be right at the feet of some blank-faced, blue-eyed dame saying, "I'm sorry, but I washed his fingerprints off the door, they were all covered with blood, it looked as if I never scrubbed." He took out his handkerchief and blew his nose savagely. Her voice, coming as through the distant roar of the Volga booming across the bosom of the Little

Mother of all the Russias, sounded thin and reedlike in his congested ears. ". . . not blunt like your shoes, but sort of . . ." And then she was standing there looking at him blank and half-dazed again.

"Isn't that funny?" she said. Her eyes wandered off across the garden to a little bunch of bamboo stalks lying on the ground by the frost-bitten chrysanthemum in the border. "That's just what it looked like. I thought there was something funny about it. It looked like the print you'd make with a pair of patent leather evening shoes."

She looked back at Carlson. "You . . . you don't suppose it could have been anybody that . . . that was at the Maynards' party? The men had on dinner coats. But that doesn't make any . . . any sense. Who would—I mean, they were all our friends, Chief Carlson!"

She twisted her fingers together quickly, the pitch and tempo of her voice rising in indignant protest. "It couldn't have been anybody who's a friend of ours!"

"It looks like the fella that killed Doc Wernitz was a friend of his," Swede Carlson said, in as matter-of-fact a tone as he could manage. "He wouldn't have been in the house if he wasn't. Nothin's turned up missin', so far, that we know of."

She was looking down at the raked patch of earth. "He was going that way." She pointed to the iron gate at the end of the narrow garden. "If he went through there, he must have got away down the alley.—Do you know what I bet, Mr. Carlson? Not bet—I don't mean that." She amended it hastily. "Because I'm never going to gamble any more. I lost over a thousand dollars on the slot machines."

She broke off, her jaw dropping, her eyes wide. She raised her hand halfway to her mouth and dropped it to her side again. "Why, I've . . . I've said it! I'm not afraid to say it any more! But . . . that's wonderful, isn't it? I've been . . . I've been too ashamed to admit it to anybody else!"

"You'll feel better, admittin' it, Mrs. Blake. I guess we all do crazy things we don't like to admit to anybody, one time or another." He let her stand there in a dazed wonder at herself an instant. "What is it you were goin' to bet? If you'd been a bettin' man, that is, Mrs. Blake."

Her face lighted up in a sudden delighted smile, and sobered as quickly. "You know Mr. Hanzenhofer? The baker over on Mercer Street?"

Swede Carlson nodded.

"Well, he runs a night shift, and he won't let any of them smoke in the kitchens. I don't think it's a kitchen at a bakery, but where they make the bread and stuff and bake it. Or any place—he's mean about it, really. So they go out in back, where there's that lattice place, where he has the grape vine. They go out there and smoke when he's not looking. And maybe—I mean, if any of them happened to be out there, and anybody went along the alley . . .

Carlson nodded again. "I'll look into it. Now, you listen to me, Janey. I'm going to call you that, because Gus is a friend of mine." He saw her stiffen, and went calmly on. "I'm goin' to wait downstairs while you go get your things and get that baby of yours. Then I'm goin' to take you down to your mother's. Now, you're not to say anythin' to anybody, about what you told me here. Not your mother, or your father, not even Gus. Hear? You're not to say anythin' about that shoe print, or anythin' else. I'm like you, Janey. I'm not easy to scare. But I'm sort of scared right now. I'm goin' to be worse scared if somebody happens to find out maybe you're not so stupid after all. You just don't say anythin' to anybody 'cept to me."

He took her arm and started back to the kitchen door with her.

"Let's look at it this way, Janey. If I'm right, and I'd be the last fella in Smith County to think I ain't, somebody came in here last night to get somethin' you all have got. Or . . . but we'll skip the other. We'll assume it's somethin' you've got he's got to get a hold of. Now you think that over, and keep your mouth shut about it. You hear. Janey?"

"Yes," Janey Blake said. "I hear. I . . . think they must be mistaken, but I . . . I still hear. I promise. I won't say a word."

She was a woman, Swede Carlson reflected, but somehow he believed her when she said it.

FIFTEEN

AT FOUR O'CLOCK Connie Maynard swung her typewriter back from the side of her desk and put the cover on it. She took one more look at the paper before she folded it, took her bag out of the drawer, powdered her nose, put on more lipstick and got up to get her coat on the hinge behind the door. She was very pleased with herself, and with the paper. It was the most exciting edition of the *Smithville Gazette* that had come off the old presses since she'd come there six months before. And she was the girl responsible for it. Gus's room was still empty. Nobody had even bothered to turn on the light. Gus had walked off, Miss Constance Maynard had taken charge without a qualm or a moment's panic. The whole thing had gone off as smoothly as anything had ever done around the *Gazette*—more so, because Gus wasn't in there snapping at people and pulling stuff and putting last-minute stuff in that wasn't of any world-shaking importance, no matter what the people of Smithville who'd called it in might think. And she'd yanked the last obituary off the front page, which was more than Gus had had the courage to do. Who cared whether some old Miss This-or-That threw in her last chip? The fact that the whole front page was a magnificent if left-handed obituary of one Doc Wernitz did not at the moment occur to her. For once, there was real news in Smithville. She put on her coat and stuck the paper in her pocket. Her father would like this.

She went out into the quiet press room, comparatively quiet with the presses closed down until Monday and everybody rushing around to get through and go home.

"Good night!" She waved her hand around generally. Gus's habit of being the last man out had always seemed to her an irritating bit of occupational egocentricity, especially when she wanted him to stop by the Sailing Club or the house and have a drink before he went home to dinner. Ed Noonan the City Editor was still at his desk, his eyes with no lashes batting every once in a while like an old lizard's on a stump in the sun. His green eyeshade was pushed back and stood up around his bald dome like an emerald halo. The country editor's alpaca coat with a hole in each elbow hung on the hook behind him. Connie frowned a little. There was too much corn flourishing around the *Smithville Gazette*. A vigorous strenuous course of contour ploughing was what the place needed.

Ed Noonan batted his old lizard eyes down. His skin was dry as a lizard's too.

"Aren't you going home, Ed?" Connie stopped to pull her gloves on.

"No. Got to stick around to meet a fellow."

"Gus?"

It was out of Connie's mouth before she knew she had said it. But before Ed could answer, if he intended to answer, which was doubtful, the storm door pushed open abruptly, the plateglass door following at

once, and Swede Carlson came in. Charged in, Connie thought, stepping
hastily back out of the way of the door.

"Where's Gus? I want to see him."

He spoke to Ed Noonan, not Connie. Ed shook his head.

"Where is he, Miss Maynard?"

Connie should have shaken her head too. She realized it on her way
home, but not at the moment. "I don't know where he is," she said. Her
voice flattened like a cobra head. "Nobody knows where he is. Nobody's
seen him since morning. He walked out of here and left me to get the
paper out all by myself. With Ed's help, of course."

She added the last, seeing the startled shift of Chief Carlson's eyes
toward the City Editor. She did not see Ed Noonan's left lid lower
slightly or the bleak flicker of response in Carlson's. "If you want Gus,
you'll have to find him," she went on. If Chief Carlson thought she'd
forgotten this morning in her office he was very much mistaken. She was
even skipping a cocktail party to go home and tell her father, and
perhaps Chief Carlson would find himself with leisure to write his ex-
periences instead of telling them to people. And he must have thought
of that himself; she could see the change taking place in him right there
by the door.

"Well, that's all right, Miss Maynard," he said. He was smooth as
anything, all of a sudden. "I guess it's you I want to see, not Gus. You
can probably tell me more than he can, if that's the way of it."

He pulled the *Gazette* out of his overcoat pocket. It was folded to the
box in the middle of the front page. "Mighty smart reportin', here." He
tapped it with a blunt forefinger. "Just where'd you get this information
about Doc Wernitz, Miss Maynard? That's all I want to know."

"That's information from private sources, Swede," Noonan said. He
lowered both eyelids and dragged at his cigarette. "You could easy take
legal steps to make us disgorge, I guess. But that'd be a lot of trouble.
Nobody here can claim the reward. I guess Gus'll tell you where he got
it soon as he comes in. I don't know, or I'd tell you. I doubt if Connie
knows either. Do you, Connie?"

"No, I don't."

"So that's the way it is, Swede." Noonan leaned back in his chair. "If
I was you and I wanted Gus, I'd do what they call a pub crawl. That's
what he looked like to me when he went outa here this morning. Like a
guy that was going to go and get drunk as hell. I don't say he did. I say
he looked like he was going to. And I'm sittin' around here because my

daughter's husband is going to come and buy me a drink or two. Stick around, both of you. He's got all kinds of dough."

Connie looked at Carlson. She couldn't tell whether Ed was lying or telling the truth, or what Swede Carlson thought about it. Their faces were at opposite poles of complete inscrutability. Carlson stuck the *Gazette* back in his pocket and moved over to the desk.

"Mind if I use your phone?"

"Go ahead." Noonan pushed it over to him. "Mind if we listen?"

"Go ahead." He dialed a number and waited, the phone pressed close to his large purple-tinged ear. "Carlson speakin'," he said. "Listen, son. I want Gus Blake. Yeah. That's right. You know Gus Blake. I want him tonight, drunk or sober. 1941 coupé, black. What's his number, Ed?" He repeated the license number in the phone. "No, I don't want him in the jail house, I want him wherever he is. Even if he's in the—" He remembered Miss Maynard. "—in the library readin'. I want to talk to him. Hear? Relay this to Williams at City Headquarters and tell him I said would he put his men on it. Hear? Get on it, son. I want to talk to him before somebody finds him and cracks him over the skull too. And I'm not foolin', hear?"

"He must unless he's stone deaf," Connie said lightly.

Chief Carlson put down the phone. "Well, I'll shove along, Ed." He went to the door. "If you see, Gus, Miss Maynard, tell him I'm lookin' for him. Hear?"

As he went out, Connie turned sharply to Noonan. "Where is he? I've *got* to know!"

Noonan pushed his chair back, its top edge resting in the groove in the plastered wall behind him. "If anybody else asked me that question, Connie, you know what I'd do?" he said dispassionately.

"No. What?"

"I don't know myself. It would all depend. But don't you ever ask me another question like it."

He crossed one foot over his knee and held it with both hands, whether from custom or for purposes of self-restraint, Connie couldn't tell.

"In this business you don't lie, Connie—especially not to the cops. If they ask you a direct question, you give 'em a direct answer. If you don't know, you say so. If you know and can't tell, you say that. You don't do one thing and say the other. If you do, first thing you know you're out in the snow right flat on your royal white palfrey—and try to find some news from them that's fit to print or anything else. Good night, Connie.—Hear?"

"Sorry."

She opened the door. Ed Noonan's grating voice stopped her halfway through it. "Maybe there's one more thing I could say before you go, Connie." He teetered forward and back again, still holding on to his foot. When Swede Carlson says he wants Gus before somebody cracks him on the head, he ain't kiddin'. Swede don't have time for the funny papers."

Connie's lips tightened. She shut the door quietly behind her. Gus Blake could take care of himself without any help. If Gus wouldn't stick his neck out far enough to offend people by keeping their obituaries off the front page, he was hardly likely to stick it out so far he'd get his skull crushed in. Gus was smarter than most people thought. How psychic did Ed Noonan think he was?

She got in her car, switched on the motor and let off the brake.

"Home, Connie," she said deliberately. "Home. You've been kicked around enough today."

She left her car in the drive in front of the house and hurried up across the wide white-pillared porch to the door. She hoped John Maynard was at home. She needed somebody to re-establish her battered ego. And he was there. She could see him through the narrow slit where the green-gold curtain had been carelessly drawn at the library window. He was pacing slowly back and forth in front of the fire, his hands in his pockets, his head bent down, lips moving, heavy brows pulled together in concentrated furrows. Connie frowned. That meant his frazzle-haired giraffe-lipped old maid secretary was there. The only time John Maynard ever paced, eyes on the floor, was when he was dictating.

Connie stopped a moment in the hall, listening for the low rich mellow rumble of his voice. She cocked her ear more intently. He must be almost through. She waited for Miss Delabear's high-pitched nasal voice to come clacking through the door.

"That's funny," she thought. She heard the phone ring in the pantry and cocked her ear the other way. It might be Gus calling her. Her pulse quickened at the thought, and slowed again as she heard the buzzer in the library, heard the chair knock against the desk and her father's friendly drawl as he answered. Her face brightened. He was alone, then. She took the paper out of her pocket, took her coat off and laid it over the mahogany newel post, and gave herself a cursory glance in the mirror behind the banked chrysanthemums, waiting a moment for him to finish before she went over and opened the library door, the paper in her hand. She hoped he hadn't seen it yet. He usually waited for her to bring it home.

"Hi," she said, smiling gaily. He was just putting down the phone, and not smiling till he saw her. Then his handsome face composed itself into its customary bland and amiable lines.

"Hello, Connie honey," he drawled. "How's my girl?"

There was something missing. She felt it in the atmosphere more than she saw it in her father's face or heard it in his voice. Her own warm anticipatory pleasure chilled.

"What's the matter, Daddy?"

Her eyes fell on the *Gazette* spread out on the desk in front of him. His hand was still on the phone. He reached out, pressed the bell under the edge of his desk and took the phone up again.

"Lawrence," he said, "I've gone out if any one else calls the next couple of hours or so." He put the phone down and smiled at his daughter. His facial muscles smiled, she realized. The youthful brown eyes fixed on her had failed to get the word.

"Nothin's the matter, Connie," he drawled pleasantly. "Just a mite wore out tellin' people to call Gus, not me, and havin' them tell me they already called Gus. Where is Gus, by the way, Con?"

She felt an unaccountable relief. "Golly, Daddy." She came across the room and flopped down in the deep leather chair by the desk. "I was afraid for a minute it was me you were mad at. I don't know where Gus is. He came in looking like a cross between Mussolini and a rattlesnake and barged out, leaving me to get the paper out. I thought I'd be panicky about it, but I really wasn't. That's what I dashed home to tell you. I thought you'd be pleased with me."

A mildly humorous light twitched in her father's eyes for an instant and disappeared. He glanced down at the front page of the paper.

"I'm mighty pleased, honey," he drawled. "Where was old Ed, all the time? He barge off, too?"

"No, Ed was there." The warm tingle in Connie's cheeks sharpened her voice. "But I was responsible. Even if he did write the leaders. I'm not pretending I ran the presses and made all the deliveries either."

"Keep your shirt on, Con," John Maynard said mildly. He tapped the box in the center of the front page. "Where'd Gus get all this about Wernitz, honey? You any idea? It's mighty interestin' to me."

"None at all. You're the second person who's asked me that."

The flush in her cheeks deepened. "Chief Carlson was fit to be tied."

"He was? Well, that's interestin' too. So at least Gus didn't get it from him, did he, Connie?" He folded the pages. "I expect Gus don't want to tell anybody just where he did get it. Ever thought of that, honey? That maybe that's why he didn't stick around very long today?"

"Oh," Connie said. "Oh." She hadn't thought of it. And maybe that did explain it. With what old Ed had told her about direct answers to direct questions, and legal methods making people talk who didn't want to talk, that could very well be it.

"But maybe not," her father added as he saw her eyes brighten. "Gus is an unpredictable sort of feller, in my experience with him. I wouldn't draw any conclusions, myself."

He put his chin down on his shirt collar and folded his hands across his stomach, his elbows resting on the arms of his chair. After a moment he looked up.

"Carlson's trying to find Gus?"

Connie nodded. "He's got the whole force out after him. He was trying to scare me and Ed into telling him where Gus had got to. He said somebody might try to cave Gus's skull in too."

"That so?" John Maynard said. "Well, Carlson's supposed to be a pretty level-headed sort of fellow. I expect he knows what he's doing."

"Oh, rot!" Connie snapped. "Carlson's a . . . a half-wit, if you want to know my personal opinion of him. He came in the office—"

Her father nodded. "I know. He told me he was in talkin' to you."

"He did?" She let the cigarette she'd reached for drop back into the box. "Did he tell you what he said to me? Practically accusing *you* of murdering Wernitz? Swindling him out of his property and then killing him to save your own reputation? Did he tell you that's what he said to me?"

She straightened her body up in the leather chair and got to her feet. "He didn't have the guts to tell you that, I'll bet."

"—Sit down, Constance," John Maynard said.

She dropped abruptly back in the chair. Her mouth dropped open a little. Neither his voice nor the smiling lines on his face had changed, but everything else had. She tried stupidly to remember when he'd called her Constance before. Not for years. Not since she was fifteen and had called her mother a liar at the dining-room table.

"Sit down and listen to me, honey."

His voice reached her across a dazed stretch of intense and breathless silence. A stranger was speaking to her. Under the outward guise of familiarity and friendliness, a stranger was sitting at her father's desk, as impenetrable as bed rock, a whiplash concealed in his slow mellow drawl.

SIXTEEN

"WHEN I SAID you had brains, maybe it wasn't brains but imagination I was talkin' about," she heard the stranger say. "Imagination's all right, except when it gets too powerful and goes off the track unless there's brains behind it to keep it where it belongs. The trouble with you, honey, is you're like a hound dawg in the spring time. You ain't usin' the brains you got, daughter. You're figurin' you're Constance Maynard, so let everybody else go to hell and stay there. You ain't thinkin' about nobody else but Constance Maynard. When people start doin' that, Connie, they're licked before they leave the post. That's a mistake. You're makin' a gawdam fool of yourself, Connie, and I just hate to see it, honey. Swede Carlson knew you was doin' it. So does everybody else."

"Swede Carlson!" She sat up again, her eyes blazing. "What did he come to the office for? What was he trying to pump me about your deal with Gus about the paper for? What—"

"Just for the pleasure of seein' you get in a swivet of some kind or other, honey, I expect," John Maynard said gently. "Just to see what you did and didn't know."

"He saw all right then. Because I don't know. I don't know anything. I don't even know why he should come straight to you the minute Doc Wernitz gets killed. Or why—"

"Because I happen to know more about Doc Wernitz's affairs than most anybody else in Smith County, Connie." John Maynard pushed his chair back from the desk. "Anybody but one man. And Swede Carlson." He got up to his feet. "I didn't realize Doc Wernitz was the sort of fella to take the Chief of Police into his confidence when he was gettin' up ready to pull out of Smithville. It might 'a made a considerable difference if he'd been a little more communicative, in fact, Connie. It ain't always a good plan to keep too many things to yourself. For instance . . ."

He hesitated an instant. "I don't much like to jump to any conclusions, but it's my guess that if Wernitz had told everybody he wasn't really pullin' out of Smith County, all he was doin' was pullin' out of the gamblin' end of it, because he'd made all the money he could ever use, and no family or relatives left any place for him to leave it to . . . and time runnin' out fast before the big boys decided Smithville was fat enough territory for them to move in . . . if he'd told people that, I expect he might still be alive and enjoyin' the sunshine down in Florida this winter, instead of bein' down there in the dark like he is. He was always funny about the dark. Didn't like it much. Hated it like sin and Satan, you might say if you wanted to tell the truth. So that's why Carlson came to see me, honey."

"But why not?" Connie thought. After all, why not? Why shouldn't her father know all about Doc Wernitz's business. Her father was a lawyer. Lawyers didn't pick their clients because they liked their table manners, or refuse them when they didn't. He probably had a lot of people he did business for that he let in the back way. She was suddenly aware of her father's eyes studying her face, and the amusement in them. Transparent again, no doubt. Just as Swede Carlson had said.

"Not that it's any of your business, honey," John Maynard said. "Don't start gettin' your little back up again, because it don't do anybody any good. Tomorrow I'm goin' out to Wernitz's with Carlson and Hugo Vanaman to look through his papers. Most people think Vanaman ain't as savory a character as he might be, but he's a smart lawyer. Wernitz used him where a savory character mightn't 'a done the trick. Then maybe we'll know more'n we know right now."

"You mean you don't really know too much yourself?"

"That's right," John Maynard agreed amiably. "Might say I don't know nary a single blessed thing, in fact. So you just run along now. Jim Ferguson's comin' in a few minutes to talk about some business."

"Dad." She'd forgotten about the bank and Janey's checks, and what her cousin Dorsey had told her. It flashed back now. "Why did you do it? Why did you have to go and cover Janey's checks? Why didn't you find out who stole them and make them—"

She put her hand up to her mouth and involuntarily took a step backwards. "I . . . I'm sorry. I'm sorry, Dad." She should never have let him know she knew about the checks—not because of her promise to Dorsey, which was unimportant, but because of himself . . . because of the way he was looking at her again. She shivered a little and moved back another step.

"Who told you I covered Janey's checks, honey?" His voice, still unchanged, stopped her before she could take the step that would get her to the door. She shivered again. "—But don't tell me." He went on before she could speak. "You probably weren't supposed to tell me anybody told you, were you, Connie?"

She shook her head.

"You talk too much, honey," John Maynard said equably. "You got too much gab. Maybe some day you'll learn. But you listen to me now—listen and keep your mouth shut. I know who took Janey's checks. I know who took them, and where they are."

He stopped a moment to let it sink into her bewildered brain.

"Now that's enough, Connie. Enough and plenty. You go get yourself dressed. Decently dressed, I mean. Not that green rig you had on last night. It didn't do you any good then and tonight you won't need it. I don't expect Gus is going to show up at the Sailing Club tonight. And the others'll be coming—"

"Others? What others? I'm not going to the Sailing Club tonight. I'm not going anywhere."

John Maynard looked at the clock again.

"You're going to the Sailing Club tonight, Connie. You wouldn't want anybody to think you were all up in the air about what Swede Carlson told you, would you? Or tell people you'd got yourself so all worked up you forgot—"

"Oh," Connie said. She had forgotten.

"You forgot you invited Jim and Martha Ferguson, and Dorsey and Gus, to dinner tonight, while Janey was saying goodby to your mother, didn't you? I expect you remember it now. You remember Gus said he had to go to the Town Meeting—so you invited Orvie to come and take Janey to the Sailing Club. So you could cut and go with Gus—or drop in at the Town Meeting after he got there. Well, you did it. And your mother invited your Aunt Mamie and your Uncle Nelly. Your mother's a kind woman, Connie. She don't like to see people be rude to anybody right in front of their faces, like you were to Aunt Mamie. Askin' Dorsey right after Mamie had asked him to go to the Town Meetin' with her when Gus mentioned it."

"I'm sorry. I guess I didn't hear her ask him." Connie moved over to the door.

"I'm sure you didn't, honey. You were thinkin' about yourself, not an old fool like Mamie. That's what I've been tellin' you. And somethin' else, Connie." He reached over and tapped the front page of the paper on the desk. "I'd just put down the phone when you came in. Well, it was the fifth time people had called me up, because they couldn't get hold of Gus and old Ed had told 'em to call you. They called me instead."

Her face was a blank as she looked at him and down at the *Gazette*.

"Old Miss Mattie Lewis that died last night had a lot of friends here in Smithville, honey. More'n I've got, and a heap more'n you've got or will have, the way you're startin' out not to make 'em. Miss Mattie's family have lived in Smithville a long time. More folks in Smithville are interested in readin' about Miss Mattie, and who her ancestors were, and about them givin' the land for the Church and the Park, and startin' off the first hospital, than care anythin' about whether Doc Wernitz is alive or dead. They figure Miss Mattie did more for them than the fellas that operate or play the slot machines. And it was you, Ed tells me, that stuck her notice over on the back page. Gus never would 'a done that, honey. He's got some kind of a heart inside him. That's one of the reasons he's a first-rate editor of a small-town newspaper. So run along, now—but you better try to think of somethin' to tell your advertisers as well as your readers when they cancel on Monday. I told 'em it was out of respect for Miss Mattie—we didn't want it alongside a murdered gambler. You take it on from there."

Connie heard Lawrence opening the front door for Jim Ferguson. "Hello, Jim," she said. "Dad's waiting in the library."

Her father's final comment was still in her inner ear. "I'm not just bein' hard on you, honey. I'd just like to beat a little sense into your pretty little fool head." It was still there halfway up the stairs when she heard another car drive into the yard. She glanced at her watch. It was twenty-five minutes to six. Only an hour and thirty-five minutes since she'd left her desk to come home full of congratulatory self-pride. There's darn little of it left now, she thought dismally, waiting there for Lawrence to answer the door bell. It could be Gus, but she had begun to doubt any of her intuitions. They seemed always to turn out to be wishful thinking, doomed from scratch. Then her hand casually resting on the mahogany banister contracted sharply on it. She recognized the voice at the front door, stepped back down a couple of steps and leaned over.

"Tell Chief Carlson my father is in a business conference," she said curtly. "He can wait down in—"

"He wants to see you, Miss Connie. Not your father."

"Me? What does—"

She caught herself a second time. "Very well. Tell him to come in."

She turned and went down the stairs. If Chief Carlson wanted to see her he could; but she was on her own territory now and she'd been pushed around all anybody was going to push her for one day. The fleeting glimpse she caught of herself in the chrysanthemum-banked mirror showed a young woman of confidence, tight-lipped and determined.

"What is it, Mr. Carlson?"

"I'd like to talk to you a few minutes, if you don't mind, Miss Maynard."

"Very well," Connie said. She waited in the middle of the hall. "We're having guests for dinner, so I hope it will be a few minutes. Go ahead."

"I'd just as soon talk to you here," Swede Carlson said agreeably. "But I think maybe you'd prefer it was a little more private."

Her brows slanted upward. "I'm sorry. My father's in the library and our guests will be in the living room very shortly. There's no place else, Mr. Carlson."

"That game room of yours?"

As she hesitated he added affably, "I'd like a look at it anyway, if you don't mind. Understand you had a party down there, last night."

She nodded. He wasn't going to call her transparent a second time. *Keep your temper, Connie.* She drew the door into the back hall open. If he wanted to see the play room, he should have had her father show it to him when he was there before, but it would look odd if she refused to let him see it now.

"Down here," she said. She opened the door to the cellar steps and switched on the light. It looked bare and cavernous without a fire and with no people there. She led him down. "This is it," she said curtly. "Will you sit down?" She took a match off the mantelpiece, put it to the Cape Cod lighter and stuck it under the newly placed logs. The room smelled like a bar and stale tobacco smoke still permeated it. It always took a couple of days to air out after a party in the winter.

She sat down on the yellow leather sofa, formally erect, her hands folded in her lap. "All right. What is it? I hope you're not going to give me any more—"

She stopped.

"Any more of that corny rigmarole like this morning?"

He looked at her coolly.

"I just got a lecture on being rude, but if you want to put it that way, it's fine."

Swede Carlson's bleak colorless eyes still rested on her.

"I'll make it very short, Miss Maynard. I've just got one single question to ask you. Last night, when you were all upset, you insisted on Gus goin' home right away. Why? That's all I want to know."

Connie Maynard's eyes widened involuntarily. Whatever she was ready for, this was not it.

"Why, I . . . I thought I told you." She caught herself sharply. "We talked—"

"I know we talked about it this mornin', Miss Maynard. That was part of the corny rigmarole. Now we're down to some brass tacks. You put on quite a show out there. Now I don't pretend to be much of a psychologist. That's corny too. But let's say I figure it this way. You had somethin' eatin' you, out there last night, Miss Maynard. Sittin' out in the dark alone in your car, it got worse instead of better. One of my boys said when he went out to give you your father's message, you acted like you'd seen a ghost. He was sorry he scared you, but he thought you must have seen him come out the door."

"But that's . . . that's silly," Connie said warmly. "It's all a lot of cockeyed nonsense. He didn't startle me."

"Look, Miss Maynard." Swede Carlson's smooth country voice caught a tough undertow. "I know a scared woman when I see one. What I want to know is why were you scared. You've heard of accessories before and after the fact, haven't you, Miss Maynard?"

"Of course I have." Her cheeks flushed, her eyes snapped like the chestnut logs in the fireplace.

"Okay then. You wanted to get the hell away from there. The worst way. You were tired. You had to go home. But you didn't go home. You didn't drive home and let Gus walk. You took Gus to his house. You went in with him and stuck around. You—"

"Oh. Janey, I suppose. You've been talking to Janey Blake."

"That's right. I've been talkin' to Janey Blake. I'm talking to you right now. I want to know why it was so damned important for you to get to the Blake house last night."

"—And wouldn't you be surprised if I told you." She didn't say it aloud. "—It would give you another idea about little pansy-faced Janey." Then she felt a small cold hand touch her, warning her. It would give Swede Carlson another idea about her too. She realized it sharply. Or maybe that was what he meant by accessory. If she knew Janey meant to kill herself and hadn't tried to stop her. . . . She moistened her lips with the tip of her tongue. But he couldn't have known about her . . . and Janey hadn't killed herself anyway. This was a trap. He was on the other side of the political fence from her father. He was just trying to get something he could put away to use later. She blanked her eyes, looking at him steadily across the white rug between the sofas on either side of the fireplace, and shook her head.

"I have no idea what you're talking about," she said calmly. "It was just atmosphere, out there. It got me down. When I got away from it I felt all right. The lights were on at the Blakes'. I thought maybe some of our guests had dropped in on Janey and I could use a drink too. That's all there is to it."

"I wonder, Miss Maynard," Swede Carlson said. "I hear a lot of people talkin' around about things that aren't any of their business. But they still talk, and usually there's a good deal of truth mixed in what they're sayin'. You can throw me out if I'm wrong, but the idea I get is that all things bein' equal, you'd a damn sight rather spend the time alone with Gus Blake than with his wife and your guests. You left them mighty quick, last night, I hear, to go out with him to Wernitz's. And if you figured they were in there, you must 'a figured one of 'em would take you home and not Gus."

"Aren't you being rather insulting, Mr. Carlson?" Her yellow-green eyes contracted slowly as she looked across at him.

"I'm just tellin' you the local gossip. If it's insultin', don't blame me. I've been watchin' you, Miss Maynard. The way I figure you is that you know what you want and you go after it. Fair means or foul. And then you get sort of scared. Or maybe your conscience gets to botherin' you. A lot of women are like that."

"Are they indeed, Chief Carlson?" She lifted her perfect brows. "You've learned a lot about people, haven't you? May I ask what you think my reason for going to Blakes' was?"

"Sure," Swede Carlson said. "Glad to tell you. In view of what happened there last night I figure you knew somebody was goin' to break in the Blakes' house. I figure you knew who it was and why they were doin' it. That's why you weren't interested in the phone call out there at Wernitz's. Maybe you'd agreed to keep Gus away long enough for 'em to go in and do what they were goin' to do. I figure that sittin' out there in the car, your conscience began to hurt like hell. You saw what murder was like, and it suddenly began to worry you . . . that who'd ever killed once could easily kill again. And I think that's when you got what you call upset, Miss Maynard. That's why you had to get Gus home so fast all of a sudden. I think that's why you went inside when you got there—just to see what had happened. And when you found Janey alive, and you got all over your jitters, you started right back on the same track again.—Does that answer your question, Miss Maynard?"

Connie Maynard had straightened up and was sitting rigidly erect on the yellow sofa, her dry lips parted, listening in a stupor of stunned fascination to the fantastic compound, half of it falsehood, half truth. It was a ghastly net, being woven right in front of her . . . the truth as damning as the falsehood, the falsehood as damning as the truth.

SEVENTEEN

SHE MADE HERSELF stare calmly and steadily back at him. As she let herself back against the leather sofa, the air forced out of the cushions covered the sound of her own slowly escaping breath.

"You must be joking, Chief Carlson." She spoke as evenly as she could.

"I'm not joking and you know I'm not."

He watched her intently. He'd scared her, scared the living daylights out of her. There was something in it, then. In what part of it? What the hell was this woman really up to? Somewhere in what he'd said he'd scored a bull's-eye. She'd folded her hands in her lap again and crossed her elegant legs. She probably didn't realize she'd uncrossed them abruptly when he'd said her conscience had begun to bother her, out there in the car in Wernitz's yard. But she was getting herself together again. There was even a queer mirthless quirk at one corner of her mouth. Swede Carlson thought coolly. He hadn't got all of what she was up to, in what he'd said, but he'd got part of it.

"Is something funny, Miss Maynard?" he asked deliberately.

"Yes. Or no. It depends. It's not funny at all, really." She got to her feet. "I do a kind act for a gal whose husband you think I'm trying to swipe, and I end up a suspect in a murder case. An accessory before or after, whichever way you take it. Is that funny? It doesn't seem terribly funny to me. But I've had a rough day, so maybe I just don't quite see it. If you haven't any more—"

She broke off, the color flooding back into her cheeks, as his bleak gaze moved away from her and rested on the slot machine in the far corner of the room. "And if you're wondering where—"

She stopped again, turning quickly to the staircase. It was not her father, as she half expected it would be, but the house man. He was looking over the banister. "The telephone, Miss Connie. It ain't for you, it's for Chief Carlson."

"Oh." She checked her forward movement abruptly. "Over there, Mr. Carlson—behind the stairs."

As he went over, she tried desperately to collect herself and think coolly. This was awful. What in God's name could she say? *He thinks —maybe he knows—there's some connection between Wernitz's murder and the entering business at the Blakes'*. Was she going to have to tell a terrible truth, to save herself from being pilloried as an accessory to the murder of a small-time gambler that she had no connection with at all? Except, she thought quickly, that her father knew more about Doc Wernitz's business than anybody . . . anybody except the bumbling uncanny fool over the telephone under the stairs. Her mouth was dry. She tried to swallow, to secrete saliva. The taste was bitter.

Carlson came back, moving rapidly, not in his usual torpid and phlegmatic way. He took his overcoat off the sofa and thrust his arms into it, his face even grimmer and tougher than it was when he was telling her what he thought she'd been up to. It was worried too, concerned, and he hadn't been concerned at all about her.

"What is it, Mr. Carlson?"

He went over to the stairs and started up.

Her voice rose, high-pitched and urgent, in sudden alarm. "Mr. Carlson! Answer me! It's Gus, isn't it? Is he—have they found him?"

He turned halfway up the stairs. "No, they haven't found him, Miss Maynard. Found his car, turned over in a ditch. And a lot of blood. Out by Doc Wernitz's, just past Newton's Corner. They haven't found Gus yet."

His eyes flickered oddly. "Why, Miss Maynard? Why're you so worried? Did you think he was goin' to be found, some place?"

He went on up the stairs. She stood there for a moment, listening aimlessly to his heavy step in the hall.

Connie Maynard sat at the dinner table, an hour later, between Jim Ferguson and Orvie Rogers, tense and alert, waiting for the telephone to ring. Running frantically up the stairs from the cellar play room, her first impulse was to burst into the library and tell her father and Ferguson. But the door was locked. It was the first time in her life she had ever known it to be locked. Her second impulse was to grab her hat and coat and dash out to Newton's Corner. The coat she'd left on the newel post had been taken to her room, and by the time she got upstairs and into the closet to get it she had decided not to do that either. They'd call. They were sure to call her father when they found anything out. Until they did, she'd just keep it to herself. If her father thought she was such a fool, she'd show him she could do something rationally once in a while.

She looked around the dinner table. It was one thing for John Maynard to tell her what he'd said when she'd got home from the paper and gone in to see him. It was quite another for her cousin Dorsey to keep glancing from one of them to the other, now, as if he knew something was wrong between them. He was watching her now from across the table. She could have slapped the maddening smirk off his stupid face. Just because he looked like John Maynard was no reason for his always trying to act like him. If he'd been born with the Syms physique he wouldn't have had too much to strut about. She glanced up at her Uncle Nelly Syms at the head of the table at her mother's right. Uncle Nelly always blossomed under his sister-in-law's tact. She was the only person in Smithville—except Gus, of course—who bothered to listen to him expand and expatiate, as if the Smith County Treasurer's office was the Office of the United States Treasury and he was Undersecretary, instead of a doormat under Aunt Mamie's heavy if aristocratic foot.

Uncle Nelly was more than expanding now. Her mother must really be laying it on, Connie thought. Uncle Nelly looked ten years younger than he'd looked the night before when he horned in to talk to Gus about Aunt Mamie's piece for the Centennial edition. In fact, Uncle Nelly looked as if he'd hit twenty jackpots all in quick succession. He even told Aunt Mamie to shut her big mouth—in a nice way, of course, but shut up she had, so Connie didn't hear what she was going to tell Jim Ferguson about meeting Janey Blake on the way down to her mother's. Connie noticed that Mr. Fancy Pants Dorsey had seen that too. His eyes had opened wide in startled surprise until he saw her and winked at her.

He was probably holding his breath, actually, just waiting for Aunt Mamie to get hers back.

And Martha Ferguson had noticed it. Connie saw her smile at John Maynard on her right. "—What meat has this our Nelly et that he has grown so great?" she murmured. Connie felt a twinge of annoyance when John Maynard laughed as if it were really terrific. He always laughed when Martha Ferguson wanted him to. She was the only woman in Smithville he ever put himself out to amuse or was apparently amused by.

Connie glanced at her watch and shifted uncomfortably in her chair. It was almost eight o'clock. They must have found out something about Gus by now. Perhaps Janey knew.

"Why don't you try to get Janey again, Orvie?" she asked. She turned to what the *Gazette* always used to call "the scion of the Rogers millions" before Gus started calling him Orval Rogers. Orvie was sitting on her left, solemn-faced and preoccupied, eating as if his father had particularly told him always to chew his meat carefully and thoroughly.

He brightened up at once and put his fork down.

"Maybe Gus has got home. There's no reason she should just sit around—if he's going to the Town Meeting later on, anyway. You'll excuse him, won't you, Mother?"

"Surely."

Connie caught her mother's dubious glance. She was like all the rest of them. They all knew it was Gus she was thinking about, not Janey. All except Orvie, who was too nice ever to think at all. But while they might be right this time, it was for the wrong reason.

"Run along, Orvie," Mrs. Maynard said. "I tried to get Janey before dinner, but she didn't answer her phone."

"She is at her mother's," Aunt Mamie said. "I saw her take her suit-case in. She was with that Carlson man you've always had so much trouble with, John."

John Maynard smiled his bantering protest. "Well, now, Mamie. . . . How you talk. I didn't know—"

"You know very well you've never had anything but trouble with that man, and so has Nelson."

"Hush, Mamie," little Uncle Nelly said. "I've . . . I've never had any but the most cordial . . . anything but the finest co-operation with Chief Carlson."

"Sounds fine, Dad," Dorsey Syms said. "Mother must be ghost-writing for you now?"

His father looked severely at him. Uncle Nelly must really have been eating tiger-meat, Connie thought.

"Use the phone in the pantry, Orvie," Mrs. Maynard said, trying to keep the peace and help him get away.

"The poor dope," Connie thought. As he bounded up and away she caught Martha Ferguson's eye and smiled at her. Martha looked worried, she thought, wondering a little about it—not mad, as she'd looked at the party the night before.

"Is Gus out of town?" she asked.

Connie shrugged. "Nobody seems to know where he is. Of course if Janey isn't playing the slot machines any more, maybe she won't bother about the Sailing Club no matter where Gus is." She raised her voice so Orvie could hear her through the pantry door. "At least I gather she thinks it's about time for her to quit."

"That's the nice thing about slot machines." Dorsey Syms smiled at her. "People just think they're going to quit."

"I'm sure Janey Blake has never played the slot machines," Aunt Mamie said. She looked at her son severely. "Janey has too much sense and too high moral standards to throw money away gambling."

"But the slot machines ain't gamblin', Mamie," John Maynard said blandly. "You can only speak of gamblin' when the odds are such you've got at least a remote chance of winnin'."

"I call the slot machines gambling, John."

Mrs. Maynard looked at her daughter. "—Why on earth did you bring this up?" she was asking silently. She was not an irritable woman, but this was very irritating. Among other things, how on earth was she going to keep Aunt Mamie from knowing there was a slot machine in the basement play room if they all went on talking about and around it?

"Janey won, last night," Jim Ferguson said. "So it would be gambling for her, John. She might want to try her luck again tonight. It runs in streaks, you know."

"And don't forget she got that lucky piece too," Connie said. She smiled at her mother.

"There is no such thing as a lucky piece," Aunt Mamie said.

"Oh, yes, there is too." Connie smiled at Jim Ferguson. "You saw it, last night. It was a gilded quarter, didn't you say?"

"That's what it looked like," Jim Ferguson said briefly. "Did you get her, Orvie?"

He was anxious to change the subject too, apparently, and with reason, Connie thought. If Aunt Mamie should get the notion that her banker was interested in slot machines and believed in lucky pieces, Aunt Mamie was just the girl to take her accounts somewhere else, and her own plus those of her organizations was a sizeable amount of business as well as advertising prestige. She was looking at him over her champagne glass like an outraged thoroughbred. Aunt Mamie, Connie thought, always looked like a handsome horse when she was aroused.

"Can Janey come, Orvie?" Jim Ferguson was bent on getting away from the hole yawning in the ice.

"Well, she didn't want to, very much, but I persuaded her," Orvie Rogers said cheerfully. "Thanks, Mrs. Maynard." He settled back to his roast beef enthusiastically.

"Did you tell her to bring her lucky piece?" Connie Maynard inquired maliciously. She glanced at Jim Ferguson out of the corner of a bright and wicked eye. She'd forgotten about Gus for an instant. If she could get Aunt Mamie really started, the fireworks ought to be wonderful to watch.

"No," Orvie said. "Her . . ." He looked puzzled. "Oh, I know what you're talking about. Last night. No. I don't suppose she kept it, anyway."

Connie smiled at her mother again. "I don't suppose other people's lucky pieces do you any good," she said lightly. "I wonder whose it was? Has anybody asked about it, Daddy? If anybody took all the trouble of having a quarter gilded to carry around with him, I should think he'd miss it and try to figure out where he lost it."

"I don't know what you're talkin' about, honey," John Maynard said, smiling. He shook his head at her.

"It was a lucky quarter that popped out of you-know-where, Daddy."

"—All that glitters is not gold." Aunt Mamie put down her champagne glass. "It is an evil and adulterous generation that seeketh after signs."

"That's right, Aunt Mamie," Connie exclaimed. She flashed her sparkling eyes round the table. They were all really delightfully annoyed. Poor Uncle Nelly was turning a pale green, and Dorsey could have shot her. She laughed happily. The back of Jim Ferguson's neck was getting red-hot above his coat collar to where his blond hair could easily have stood a barber. Even Orvie Rogers was solemn-faced again. He chewed steadily away at his last piece of roast beef. "You're absolutely right, Aunt Mamie. That's us! We're an evil and adulterous generation. The lucky quarter's a symbol. It's a symbol of the slot machines we waste our substance on . . . the gilded stream emptying our pockets and filling Doc Wernitz's. Doc Wernitz is the one should have carried the lucky quarter!"

She stopped, laughing delightedly. "That's a wonderful idea, isn't it? Maybe it did belong to him! Maybe he made a mistake and put it in the machine himself. When was he here last, Daddy?"

"Mr. Wernitz never played the slot machines," Aunt Mamie said vigorously. "If it was in a slot machine, somebody else must have put it there."

"Oh, then it's a clue! Maybe it's a clue!"

She said it only because she saw her mother was getting ready to end this subject. The instant the words were out of her mouth she caught her breath suddenly. It was as if some one had struck her a blow in the face. Something seemed to snap and crackle in the atmosphere around the table. She had been so involved in the scene she was creating for Aunt Mamie to take over and develop in Aunt Mamie's style that she hadn't noticed till then that there was more than annoyance there in the room. There was tension, sharp and acrid as the smell of a burning light cord before the fuse blew. She straightened up in her chair, her mind working coolly in the sudden icy chill of her body.—What if that was really it? What if that was what some one was trying to get at Janey's house last night? The police thought it was Wernitz's murderer . . .

"Connie!" Mrs. Maynard's quiet voice brought her to. "We will not discuss Mr. Wernitz's—"

"Oh, but that's horrible, Connie!" Martha Ferguson burst out passionately. "That's a terrible thing for you to say!"

"And now she's said it, Lucy," John Maynard said quietly to his wife, "I guess she'd better go on.—You realize, don't you, honey, you've practically accused one of our guests last night of murderin' Doc Wernitz, and breakin' in on a defenseless girl with a little baby in the house? You realize what you're saying', don't you, honey?"

"Oh, no! I . . . I'm sorry!"

Connie shrank back in her chair. The impenetrable, implacable bed rock was there in her father's eyes again, fixed steadily on her down the length of the candle-lit table. "I'm sorry! I didn't mean any such thing. I . . . I was just joking."

"I'm not sure you were just joking, Constance." It occurred to Connie that except for her father all the men at the table that evening seemed inarticulate. Aunt Mamie turned to John Maynard. "If you do not inform the police, I shall do it myself, John. Mr. Wernitz did not play the slot machines. He assured me personally that he never put a dime in one of the things. And he also gave me two hundred and fifty dollars to help my campaign *against* the slot machines. He was more than glad to be of service in the community, he said."

EIGHTEEN

SWEDE CARLSON heard the siren as he turned into the country road past Newton's Corner. It screamed like a chorus of demon Malemutes and died off in a long reverberating wail in the cold November night. He could see the reflected glow of light over the trees, and a long white finger thrust high into the evening sky and travel down, sweeping a full circle of light and shadow as the beam from the Fire Department's truck moved searchingly over the landscape. The red light of his own car flashed on and off as his driver pressed the accelerator to the floorboards and they bounced and swerved, tearing up the graveled corduroy country road. Doc Wernitz's place was three-quarters of a mile farther on. The fire truck was in the middle of the road, the searchlight playing over the yellow marshland off to the right and over the dilapidated tobacco barn in the brown sleeping field to the left. Gus's car was in the ditch there, the four wheels where the top should have been. A shorter beam from the truck held it steadily in its yellow track.

"He got out, Chief. There's some blood around, but not too much. Jeez, just take a look at that front seat."

The driver of the ambulance parked in front of the truck pointed down at the wrecked car, and at the bloody patch on the marsh grass at the side of the ditch. "He got out there, crawled out. You can see where he climbed back up on the road and got over there."

Carlson looked at the blown rear tire with its gaping ragged hole, and at the tracks of the car careening off the dirt road. He followed the driver across to the white painted concrete culvert. There was a large bloody hand print on it.

"He got over here and sat down."

The men from the fire truck were sweeping the marsh and the dried field with the long powerful beam.

"It don't look like he's left the road anywhere, Chief. Looks like he sat here, and then got up and staggered on down thataway. The radiator's still boilin'."

The beam shot along the narrow curving ribbon toward the Wernitz entrance. It picked up and held the solemn sentinel line of black cedars leading to and concealing the low brick farmhouse where Doc Wernitz had lived and with brutal violence stopped living.

Swede Carlson got back in his car. In a smash-up like the one there in the ditch it was either a miracle or else. Your number was up, or it wasn't.

"Pull over and we'll go along," he said to the fireman by the truck. "He's probably headed for the Wernitz place. There's a telephone there. Stand by till I give you the word."

They went on and turned into the cedar-lined lane. Halfway along to the farmhouse, the red beam caught a figure lurching on toward the house. "There he is." The driver gave the car all the speed it would take. Carlson watched silently. Ed Noonan had said he was going to get drunk, and he looked it. He was staggering on, catching himself and staggering on again, until the red beam caught him. He stopped, swaying unsteadily.

Carlson was out of the car and caught him. "Blake!" He held him up, looking anxiously at his blood-smeared face. There was a gash down from his temple, the blood still dripping from it. His eyes were blurred and bloodshot, but there was no alcohol on his breath. Shock was all Gus Blake was drunk with. Carlson put his arm around him and led him to the car. He opened the rear door.

"I'm okay." Gus crawled in and sank down on the seat. "Just a blow-out. Tires no good."

"Take it easy," Swede Carlson said. "Give us a light, bub." The driver handed back a flashlight. "And some iodine and bandages." Carlson took the first-aid kit. "Wait a minute. We can save this till we get to the house. Get movin'. No—hold it a second."

He was looking intently at Gus. "You ought to be dead, but you aren't. We'll have a look at you at the place. Right now brace up, fella.

What'd you head out here for? Anythin' I ought to know before I walk in on it?"

Gus felt his head with both hands. He was still dazed, but things were gradually falling back into place. Then suddenly they all seemed to snap together. He opened his eyes, shut them and opened them again. He'd had a wreck. He was still alive. He wished in some dull and painful way that it had all been as simple as that. What did they call it? The will to death, the unconscious desire to die and be finished with it? If that was what he had been trying to do, going sixty over the lousy road back there, he should have succeeded. But he hadn't. He was still here. Swede Carlson was here. Everything was the same. Janey and Orvie were still here too. His stomach turned dark brown again and he licked his dry dirt-caked lips. They tasted of salt and grit. He got his handkerchief out and spat the stuff out of his mouth.

"I'm okay," he repeated. He tried to think. "I was following a guy, trying to catch up with him. Vanaman. You know Vanaman, a lawyer in town? He was supposed to be in New York making a speech tonight. Read about it in the *Gazette*. I saw him up toward Batestown, past the race track, headed this way. I thought I'd better snap out of it. He could be mixed up in it. I'm a newspaper man, see?"

He put his head in his hands again. It was splitting apart.

"He was going seventy-five, but the light got him at Newton's Corner. I saw him turn off this way. I figured Wernitz's place was the only one down here, but I didn't make it. He's up at the house now, I think. Why don't we go? I'm okay."

Carlson nodded to the driver and leaned back as the car went along the lane, thinking it over. Vanaman had showed up tonight instead of in the morning as he'd expected him to. Vanaman was a lawyer in Smithville. John Maynard and Hugo Vanaman, both lawyers, both doing business for Doc Wernitz, one on either side of the tracks, the left hand purposely vague about what the right hand was doing. So he was here now. Carlson glanced at Gus Blake leaning back in the corner. The idea he'd had that Gus had got his stuff about Wernitz from Vanaman didn't seem to hold water. But you could let that go for the moment. If Gus had met him on the highway north of the race track and he was here now, it meant he and John Maynard hadn't so far got their heads together. It would seem to indicate Vanaman wasn't as interested in talking to Maynard as Carlson had earlier got the idea Maynard was interested in talking to him.

And why the present rush? He'd been on the phone to Vanaman in New York at seven o'clock that morning. Vanaman had heard about the murder. Regretted it deeply. He was still staying on to make his speech. It was important to him. He'd be in Smithville at ten Sunday morning and meet the police and Maynard, but not till then. He'd been very firm about it. And something had happened to change his mind. It was seven-fifteen now. Making seventy-five down the express way, he could get here, New York to Smithville, in three and a half hours if he really stepped on it and wasn't caught.

The car stopped at the farmhouse, and Carlson saw Vanaman through the kitchen door. He was arguing heatedly with the policeman on guard.

"Sure, I know you're Vanaman. I know you and I know all about you. I still say you can go in and look at Wernitz's papers and all the stuff you want to as soon as the Chief says you can. That's orders. I'll call him again. You hold your horses, mister."

Gus Blake got himself stiffly out of the car and tried his feet on solid ground.

"Okay?"

"Yeah." His head ached and his voice didn't sound like much, but he was all right. He crossed the barren yard to the door.

"Hello, Vanaman," Carlson said.

The lawyer whirled around. His black hawk's eyes crackled as irritably as his sharp voice. "Chief Carlson, I demand—"

As he saw Gus Blake the change in both his face and manner was abrupt and startling.

"Why, it's Gus Blake! Why, my dear fellow, what's happened to you?" He pushed past Carlson and held his hand out. "You've been in an accident. Good God, we must—"

Gus ignored the outstretched hand. "Look, Vanaman. I don't need a lawyer. I'd have to sue myself and I can't afford it. I'm okay, it's just a scratch. Where's the bathroom, and where's that iodine?"

He went out into the back passage.

"Able fellow, Blake." Mr. Vanaman was presumably speaking to Carlson, but his voice was raised enough for it to carry through the flimsy walls. "First-rate newspaper man. A brilliant piece of reporting on the Wernitz murder. My wife read it to me over the phone this afternoon."

"Why d'you come back so fast? Thought you weren't gettin' here till tomorrow."

"No specific reason at all," Vanaman said briskly. "I just decided in general I ought to be here. Wernitz was my client, as you know. I wanted to do anything I can to help."

Carlson eyed him bleakly. "That's fine," he said. He wondered. It couldn't be the thousand-dollar reward the *Gazette* was offering. Presuming Mrs. Vanaman had read that to him too. Vanaman didn't need a thousand dollars that bad. His clients were not as respectable as those of some other Smithville lawyers, but they got in trouble oftener and Vanaman also operated the bonding company.

He glanced around at Gus coming back from the bathroom, and back at Vanaman.

"I was just telling the chief that was a brilliant piece of reporting you did, Gus." The lawyer exuded a lavish and even, it seemed, respectful cordiality that was as surprising to Carlson as it obviously was to Gus. "Brilliant," he repeated. He turned back to Carlson. "If it's agreeable to you, I'd like to check through Mr. Wernitz's desk and safe. I handled most of his affairs. I'll be able to tell you if anything's missing, and I'd like to be fully prepared for our conference tomorrow. I'll bring my records out, and if Maynard brings his, we ought to be able to give you a good picture of our end. Does that fit in with your thinking?"

Carlson nodded. "That's okay. You can spend the night here if you want to. So long as my man's in here with you and you don't take anything away you didn't bring in."

Vanaman shrugged and smiled. "Very good, Chief."

"I'd like to ask you some things about Wernitz. How well did you know him?"

"Personally, not at all," Vanaman said instantly. "You'd better ask Gus about that, not me. The details in the *Gazette* were all news to me. I made some effort to find out more about the man and got told off quick. Mr. Wernitz made it clear that business was business. So I did as I was told and kept my mouth shut. I was well paid and that was the end of it."

"You've been in this house a good deal, I guess?"

"Twice before tonight. I came in the other back door, went into his office and back out again. I came once when he'd got some bad sea food and was afraid he was going to die. The other time was last week when he called me out here to tell me he was shutting up shop and leaving Smithville."

"Did he tell you why he was leaving?"

Vanaman's bright nervous eyes focused obliquely on the floor for a moment. "I could regard that as a privileged communication," he said. He glanced over at Gus Blake propped against the kitchen table. "It's off the record. It's one of the reasons I was in New York. Mr. Wernitz was a . . . a curiously timid man. As long as the coin-machine business stayed reasonably small, he was all right. But it was getting too big, and getting too much publicity, to suit him. In May alone, he paid $49,500 to the County in license fees."

The bright hawk's eyes shot from one to the other of them.

"I imagine you know this is big business now. The pin ball and slot machine take in this county last year was something just under three million dollars. Wernitz operated most of the machines. And Smith County is small pickings. I don't know if you've read the Crime Commission's report that the slot-machine gross is three billions a year in this country. Well, now that the race track's moved in the next county, it's just a step before the big operators will move in here. We had an offer—perfectly legitimate, no threats or broken windows or anything of the sort—and Wernitz decided he'd make enough money and he'd be safer out of the business. He was right on both counts. He had . . . I may say, very large investments; he could live luxuriously if he wanted to. I was to arrange the sale of his machines, which I did, and the check's deposited to his account. It had nothing to do with his murder, Chief Carlson. I'm sure of that. It was done very quietly . . . and for precisely that reason."

"He wasn't selling any of his other interests in town?"

"Certainly he wasn't. That was the point of his retiring. He was even planning to come back here in the spring. He didn't actually say that, but I understood it."

Mr. Vanaman's thin lips smiled. "As you can easily find this out, I might tell you he held a mortgage on a house here in town that he was letting ride for exactly that purpose. It was the . . . the only evidence of malice I ever saw in him."

"Malice?" Swede Carlson said. "Whose house is it?"

"The malice was directed toward a certain lady who's made a great deal of public noise on the subject of slot machines. Wernitz was naturally opposed to publicity, in spite of the odd fact that he—"

He checked himself abruptly, glancing obliquely over at the kitchen table, not directly at Gus Blake. "I mean, he felt the less said about the machines the better. Of course, the lady in question is not aware Mr. Wernitz held her mortgage."

"She had to sign it, didn't she?" Gus asked.

"Of course. But she is a very busy lady. She signs her name a great deal. I'm quite sure her husband felt she'd prefer not knowing. And I'm very sure he preferred almost anything to having her, or his son, or his brother-in-law, know he was in debt to the extent that he was. Of course, as long as Wernitz operated the machines and the husband I'm referring to issued the County licenses, things went along very nicely. Don't misunderstand me. The husband is a very honest man. He could probably have made a great deal of money if he hadn't been. Or perhaps his connection with Mr. Maynard made it impossible. They are all very highclass people."

"Uh-huh," Swede Carlson said. "Okay, Vanaman. We've got things to do." He nodded to the policeman. "Look after Mr. Vanaman, George. He doesn't want to take anything away he didn't bring with him, so he won't mind leavin' his briefcase out here in the hall, I expect."

Outside, he beckoned to his driver. "You stay here along with George, bub. Watch the old one-two."

They got in the car. "I'm not sayin' George wouldn't resist a blandishment or two," he said. "I'm just sayin' I wouldn't trust my own Aunt Sally, in this deal." He switched the engine on and looked at Gus. "Better?"

"It smells better out here, if that's what you mean." Gus wiped his hand on his pants leg. It still felt clammy from Mr. Vanaman's parting grip that got home before he could side-step it. "What's the angle here, Vanaman and I're such good friends? I only know the guy by sight and reputation.—Give his regards to my charming wife. What's she been doing—playing the slot machines? Or is the guy going to need the press? If he is, I should have told him I'm like Wernitz. I'm getting out of Smithville too."

"Nuts," Swede Carlson said. He turned the car down the cedar lane.

"Or did Aunt Mamie slug Wernitz? Is that what he's driving at?"

"Shut up and let me think a minute." He slowed down turning into the country road. The ambulance and Fire Department truck had gone. Bub must have given the word. The countryside was silent and unpopulated as an abandoned graveyard.

"Listen to me, now," Swede Carlson said. "Things have been happenin' while you been off nursin' your hurty feelin's today. So brace

yourself, fella. I'm goin' to let you have it, straight. You don't know
what's goin' on closest to you. Your wife waited up last night to tell you,
but you came in with Connie Maynard so she was too hurt, or too mad,
to say anythin'. Don't ask me why women do the things they do. Or men
either. If the City cops would report to the County cops, or vice versa,
you wouldn't have barged off this morning before anybody could tell
you."

"Tell me what?"

"That the Wernitz killer was in your house last night . . . while you
were gallivantin' around with the Maynard girl.—I said listen to me,
Blake."

NINETEEN

THEY WERE IN TOWN when he finished. "So that's it, fella," he said.
On the whole Gus had taken it better than he'd thought at first he was
going to. "You can tell me to keep my big nose out of your private life,
and that's okay. But right now your private life's got mixed up with the
public's. My job's to find out who killed Wernitz and see he damn well
don't kill anybody else. Turnin' off the light in the basement's a dead
giveaway. It's a pattern he's thought up, it worked once, he tries it again.
He's slugged twice and I don't want him tryin' that again either. Okay.
So why was Connie Maynard in such a blisterin' hurry to get back to
your house right after it happened? I got to know that, and I got to
know what there is in your house anybody wants that bad. And one
thing more you can tell me. I figured you got your dope about Wernitz
in the evenin' paper from Vanaman, but I guess now you didn't. Where'd
you get it?"

Gus came up out of the dregs of something that hurt worse inside than
all his cuts and bruises hurt on the outside. The evening paper. It seemed
a million light—or dark—years away. It was less than twelve hours since
he'd barged out of the office and driven up one country road and down
another, trying to get rid of the gnawing rat-toothed thing eating his
insides out. And not a lot more than twelve hours since he wrote the brief
history of Doc Wernitz for the day's paper. It seemed a long time ago as
he tried to pull it back.

"Give, Blake."

"I got it from a friend of Wernitz's. His only friend, I guess. Janey's father, Swede. You needn't get sore. I didn't think of it till I was walking back from the Maynards' at three o'clock this morning. It must have been something he said some time that stuck in my mind. I decided to go take a chance on it. That's all. It paid off." He paused a moment. It hurt the side of his head to talk so much. "I don't know whether you know Janey's father. He's a queer kind of duck himself, sort of solitary, silent guy that likes being a night watchman. Orvie Rogers got him a better job once but he didn't like it. He didn't like it during the war when they ran a night shift. He and Wernitz were friends. Wernitz used to come out there and do the rounds and sit out on the pier and chew the fat with him, every time the moon brightened the place up. He didn't come unless there was bright moonlight. They got along fine, Janey's father said. He's Czech descent and Wernitz was born there. That was the bond, originally."

"I'll be damned," Carlson said.

He turned the car into Locust Street and drew up in front of the Blakes' house. It looked even narrower and smaller with no light in the windows, lonely like a shabby deserted child. He put on the brake and switched off the engine.

"Let's get on with it, Gus. I'll go in while you change and clean up, and then we're going down and talk to Janey.—And I've already told you to shut up. If you and Janey want to fight that's your business. But you don't want her killed, Gus. That's what worries me."

Gus unlocked the door and switched the hall light on.

"Go on and get cleaned up. There's a little job outside here I want to look at."

Swede Carlson went through the dining room and kitchen and let himself out at the back door. He wanted to look at the footprint the colored boy had planted grass seed over, and he also wanted to give Gus a chance to go through the misery of the abandoned bedroom and nursery by himself without anybody watching him. He shook his head. He hadn't been actively in love for so long he'd forgotten about it, how hard it could hit a guy. It looked as if it was hitting Gus Blake for the first time. And it was a laugh in some ways. A guy falling in love with his own wife, with somebody like the Maynard witch in the background. . . . It was a pretty left-handed way of doing things.

He turned his flashlight on the damp patch by the border, and nodded approvingly. It was a neat job. The loose soil from the bottom of Janey's compost heap that the kid had spread over the washed surface of the ground had been painstakingly brushed off, the under surface watered down. It was some of Lieutenant Williams's fancy F. B. I. stuff, Williams's idea, and it had paid off. Which was more than Janey's hunch about the bakery had done. The old man had spent the night there himself on a special order, so that nobody had got out to smoke a cigarette in the grape arbor. And more than the boy Buzz Rodriguez he'd been counting on had done, Carlson thought. He was conscious and he was going to be all right, but he knew less about Doc Wernitz's affairs than Swede himself knew. He looked down at the print. A substantial amount of it was left. There were a few white specks where the cast had chipped a little where the edges of the print had been raked. It was a right foot, running as Janey had said, size about 11½, thin leather sole, narrow, pointed toe and narrow heel. It could be an evening shoe as Janey had said. Tomorrow they'd find out.

He jerked around and had started running for the house even before he was certain it was Gus's voice shouting at him from upstairs. The gooseflesh was sharp as splinters of ice up and down his spine. He dashed through the kitchen. But it couldn't be. Janey couldn't have come back, not after he'd told her she had to stay away and why. He slowed down and took a deep breath of relief as he heard Gus again. "Come up here. Take a look at this." Gus was puzzled and excited, but that was all. Carlson went up the stairs. He hadn't actually realized until then, he was thinking, what a crawling feeling of horror the switched-off lights there in the night had given him, or how positive the conviction in his mind was that the hand that had turned them off was the hand that had beaten the life out of the little gambler in the house out at Newton's Corner.

"Have a look at this." Gus was waiting for him in the hall on the third floor. He had switched on the light in the front bedroom, and went back into it as Swede Carlson joined him. "It's a shambles."

"Wait a minute." Carlson stopped him at the door. They stood there looking around. "That's Janey's?" He nodded toward the dressing table in the corner by the window.

"Sure."

It was torn apart as completely as any dressing table could be torn apart. Even the box of face powder had been dumped out on the glass surface. The jewel box with its string of pearls, clips and small trinkets was dumped out. The drawers had been emptied on the floor and the contents left there.

"—Janey's coats?" He pointed to two coats with their pockets turned inside out, on the bed nearest the closet. Gus nodded. Carlson looked on around the room. The drawer in the night table between the beds had been turned over on Janey's spread. The small top drawer in Gus's chest where he kept collar studs and cuff links had been emptied on the top. Nothing else had been touched.

Swede Carlson went across the room between the beds to the telephone, picked up the receiver and dialed a number. "—Get goin', Gus," he said. "We're in a hurry.—Lieutenant Williams. Carlson here, Bill. Good work on the print. Another job for you. At Blake's house. He's been here again. Gone through the top floor front bedroom. Maybe there's a print—he spilled a lot of face powder and it sticks like glue. If we're not here use the back door. Any dime store key'll open it."

He put down the phone. Gus was pulling a suit out of the closet.

"You got any answer to this one, Gus?" Carlson watched him get a fresh shirt out of the chest. "Janey brought something home from that party at the Maynards'. The fella killed Wernitz's got to get it back. Looks like it ties him right in with the killin'. It's somethin' small, Gus. Small enough to go in this box of powder. It's a dead giveaway, of some kind—or the killer thinks it is. He wants it bad."

Gus stopped a moment, thinking. He shook his head. "Nothing I know of. Better ask Janey."

"That's what we're doin' right now. Get goin', Gus. Time's runnin' out. What's her mother's number?"

Gus gave it to him, pulled off his tie and got out of his bloodstained shirt. He wanted to hurry, but he wanted to hear her voice. The voice he could hear over the phone was her mother's.

"She's not there, Mr. Carlson. She went to the Sailing Club."

"She go by herself?"

"No, she went with Orval Rogers. You'll find her there."

Swede Carlson's hand rested for an instant on the cradled receiver. Gus had headed silently for the bathroom. Carlson shook his head. So it was Orval Rogers he was burned up about. He listened to the water running as Gus got more of the muck off his face.

"Was young Rogers at the Maynard party?" He raised his voice so Gus could hear him.

"Yeah."

"I wish to God you'd step on it, son." Swede Carlson said that to himself. He thought about all of it. Nobody with any sense could suspect old man Rogers' son Orvie had killed a guy. "—But I ain't got any sense," Swede Carlson thought. He looked at his watch and started downstairs. "I'll wait for you in the car. Make time, will you?"

There was no doubt in Gus's mind that Janey was at the Club. Halfway up the companionway to the top deck—nobody spoke of stairs or upstairs in the bar at the Sailing Club in Smithville—he heard some dame yell, "There's Janey! Hi, sweetie!" and the pack with her take it up in full cry. It was always the way. They always acted as if Janey was Doctor Livingstone just pulled in from a year's trek in the bush. Old sorehead Blake, just in from a short trek out of the ditch. But he wasn't really sore, not at anybody but himself, that is, and he was wondering how in the hell Swede Carlson thought he was going to get Janey out of the place without anybody noticing she was gone.

"Get her out here, Gus. I'll wait in the car. Don't let anybody see you if you can help it."

—Don't let anybody notice he'd taken the fair-haired child away. Don't let anybody notice the lights had gone off. He stopped by the tub of palms in the doorway between the circular bar and the long bank of slot machines curving around the corner across the winter-barred French doors to the open deck over the water. All he had to do was look for the biggest crowd. Janey would be right there in the center of it. *Sure, you're jealous as hell, Blake, but you don't have to be a stinker too, do you?* And Carlson had also told him to keep his eyes peeled to see who else was there, who else that had been at the Maynards' party the night before, if anybody.

He saw her then. At least he saw a black velvet bow on top of some tow-colored hair as soft and shining as silk just fresh from the cocoon. He couldn't see the rest because she was over on the curving banque behind the table and a lot of people were in front of it. He saw Connie Maynard's back leaning forward on the table, Ferguson beside her, laughing too loud, needing a haircut. He felt up at the back of his own head. But then he wasn't a banker with a barber's date every other Saturday the way Fergie was. Fergie must have missed out today. John Maynard was there, his gray-white poll too magnificent for any one ever to notice whether it neded a cut or didn't. And Uncle Nelly. He was there too, but he always looked like a weed anyway. The rest of the crowd, all except Orvie, and Gus skipped Orvie in his own mind, were people he didn't know, guests and visiting yachtsmen in the Basin for the week-end, all of them, including the locals, a little high for that early. He noted it approvingly. It was a good idea . . . he could do with a drink him-self, later.

Dorsey Syms was just coming back from playing the machines. Martha Ferguson was saying, "Not a dime. Not even a cherry," as a couple of people moved out so Dorsey could get back in his place beside Janey. Dorsey on one side, Orvie on the other. It was the way it had always been. It had a special irony at the moment. It was one of the things he'd gone over too many times, batting around the country roads, trying to get away from himself and everybody else. It was one of the reasons he'd married Janey. Just to show a couple of small town hot shots they couldn't play fast and loose with a kid from the wrong side of the tracks even if her father was just a night watchman at the Rogers plant. He'd marry her and show the so-and-sos. It didn't make any dif-ference to him who he married so long as it was a girl and she didn't have buck teeth and a club foot. Blake, God's nobleman. Big-hearted Ben Blake. And he still might have been right about Dorsey Syms—if he hadn't been wrong first about Janey. And how wrong could you be about Orvie? He'd been it, whatever its degree.

But that wasn't getting Janey out to Swede Carlson. He couldn't go over and drag her out. He'd have to explain all about the cut on his face. And maybe she'd refuse to be dragged out, he thought uncomfortably. He hadn't forgotten the way she'd turned tiger-cat in the kitchen that morning.

He went over to the bar.

"Scotch, Mr. Blake?" One of the barmen reached for his favorite brand. Gus shook his head.

"No, Buck. I just want to get my wife out of there a minute. Will you go ask her if she'll come over?"

The barman was looking at the patch on his face.

"Just a scratch." Gus put his hand up to it. "I was going too fast on a bad road."

"Looked like you'd been in a razor party, there for a minute." Buck grinned and raised the hinged section of the bar. "I'll tell Mrs. Blake."

Gus watched him cross the noisy room. Something mixing up inside his stomach suddenly made his eyes twitch so that he had to swallow to get rid of a watery taste in his mouth. He was acting like a school sophomore crashing the junior prom. He knew that, but it didn't help very much as he waited, trying to look his age anyway. And there was no way at all of getting her out without anybody noticing. Buck was speaking to her. He saw everybody start, the ones with their back to him turn, the sudden movement opening up a path across to the table with Janey sitting at the end. She was bolt upright, both hands around her ginger ale, her small face already white, her lips parted a little, her blue eyes still widening, going from Mediterranean sky-blue to paler blue, gray-blue like a washed-out hyacinth. He saw her swallow, loosen her fingers twined around the glass and get up, rigid as a wooden doll.

They all started moving then. Connie first. She was halfway across the room to him before Orvie and the others on the banque between Janey and the end could move to let her past. And then it happened. She wasn't coming. Gus saw her eyes flash from him to Connie and turn pitch-black, smudges like soot above her high pale cheekbones that were not pale now but a slow bright pink as she stayed where she was, just getting ready to sit right square back down again. Gus held up both hands to stop all of them. Not only Connie but Martha Ferguson and John Maynard were heading for him. He grinned at them, waving them all back.

"It's my wife I want. Go back! The rest of you go back and have another drink!"

"But Gus—your face!" Connie cried. She started toward him again.

"My face is fine." He managed a false hearty cheerfulness. "I just pushed it against some broken glass. That's why I want Janey. I want something to eat and I want her to chew it for me. I'll bring her back and tell you all about it."

He looked past them. Janey was half down on the seat, but she was coming up again, her eyes like anxious stars. He took a deep breath. At least she cared enough to worry about him getting hurt.

"Will you come, please, Janey?"

If he hadn't made it sound as casual as he could, they'd all have seen he was begging her to come. It was the way he felt. He wanted to touch her, just once to see if she was still real. She didn't look it, moving as woodenly as she was, her lips breathlessly open.

"—Gus!" she whispered.

He took her arm. "It's nothing," he said. "I'm afraid I wrecked the car. The tires are shot."

Her hand was warm on his arm. He couldn't tell which was trembling, her arm or his hand, as he guided her out and down the stairs. She still walked like a doll, her eyes wide open, fixed straight ahead of her. At the bottom of the stairs she turned toward the dining room.

"Wait a minute, Janey," he said. "I'll get your wrap. We're not going to eat, we're going to see Swede Carlson. He's waiting out in his car. He's got something he wants to ask you."

"Oh." She stopped abruptly and stood there, her back to him, while he went over to the cloakroom and got her black velvet coat. He didn't see her eyes screwed up tight like the little Dane's when she was determined not to cry, or hear what she was saying to herself.

"Stupid, *stupid* . . . I knew it was silly. I thought it was *me*. I thought for just a minute it was me he wanted. Not Connie. I thought that was why he pushed them back. I thought it was me he wanted."

He was there with her coat, putting it around her shoulders. When he took her arm again it was as wooden as her walk. She moved it before he could really get hold of it, reached forward and pulled the door open for herself. "Where is he?" She ran outside. "I see him."

Swede Carlson's stationary figure down by the car under the willow tree looked blurred and enormous and black. It focused into shape and solidity as she ran up the drive, stumbling a little until she bunched her long skirt up in her hands and ran as fast as she could.

Carlson opened the rear door for her. "Sorry to drag you out like this, Janey. Get in, will you? We want to talk to you a minute."

She slipped across the seat as close to the window as she could and settled there in a small dark huddle, the only thing visible the heart-shaped blur of her white face. She edged deeper into the corner as Gus got in beside her. Carlson got in, closed the door and leaned over the back of the seat.

"Janey, will you think carefully about this?—What did you take away from the Maynard's party last night?"

He had intended to make some mild crack about Gus's mucked-up face, but he forgot that, seeing her come tearing along leaving Gus behind. It was still in his mind, so that for an instant he missed the small involuntary gasp she gave when he asked her what she'd taken. Or almost missed it. He sharpened his gaze, trying to make her out in the dark corner. He could hear her holding her breath and see the white blob of her fist clutching the seat, holding tightly to it. A red warning light flashed on in his mind. Something here he wasn't prepared for. This was the way Connie Maynard had reacted over there in her basement play room. That he had planned. This he had stumbled on to. Maybe the two were tied together? He moved into a more comfortable position and changed his approach.

"I been thinkin' things over, Janey," he said easily. "I got it figured this way. You must 'a taken somethin'—"

"—What if I did?"

She sat bolt-upright out of her huddle.

"It's nobody's business but mine. And I threw them away. I didn't take them. I was going to, but I didn't. I threw them down the bathroom this morning. I was going to . . . I was going to kill myself, last night. But I changed my mind. I'm . . . I'm not going to kill myself. Not for anybody! I don't care any more!"

Swede Carlson's thick hand planted itself quickly in the dark on Gus Blake's knee. "Hold it. Hold it there," it said. It felt violent protest give way to obedience and shuddering horror. Gus Blake relaxed. He sank back against the seat.—Poor devil, Swede Carlson thought. Poor devils, both of them. But there was no time now.

"Why, of course you're not goin' to kill yourself, Janey," he said as she stopped to catch her breath. "What was it you took?"

"Some sleeping pills. From Mrs. Maynard's drawer. When I was leaving. Mrs. Maynard wouldn't mind my—"

"She'd 'a minded an awful lot if you'd taken 'em, Janey."

Carlson thought fast. This was it. Connie knew. She must have seen her take them, she'd let it ride till she got out there in the dark and started thinking about it. But he didn't want to ask either Gus or Janey where Connie Maynard was when they'd started home. He'd leave that for Miss Maynard to tell. The murdering little . . . And that explained the way she blew hot and cold—hot on some reason for getting Gus back to the Blake house, cold on the attempted burglary.

"Listen, Janey," he said. "Let's forget that, right now. And you think, hard. Hear? There must have been somethin' else you took. You think what you took there with you, and what else you had when you came away. Wasn't there somethin'?"

He could see her shaking her head. "No, there wasn't! There wasn't anything else!" she said passionately. "I didn't have anything with me. All I had was my bag and my handkerchief and my lipstick and compact and two quarters. That's all I took with me. And that's all I brought home except . . . except the pills, and . . . and the thirty-two dollars and fifty cents I won on the jackpot. I know that was all, because I put the bag on the hall table and took out the money and the pills. I threw the pills on the floor, and my bag dropped . . ."

She stopped, turning her head first to the right and then to the left.

"But . . . there was something else."

She stared through the dark at Carlson.

"There was the lucky piece. It fell out on the floor when I knocked my bag off the table. The lucky piece that came out of the slot machine."

Carlson's hand was still gripping Gus's knee. He moved it slowly up and let it rest on the back of the seat. "What lucky piece, Janey?"

"I don't know. It was just a lucky piece somebody had put in the machine by mistake, I guess. It came out with all the rest of the quarters. Jim Ferguson picked it up. It was gold. You know, gilded—gold-washed, I guess you call it. He . . . he made some joke about it and put it in my bag. That's all. I don't know who it belongs to."

Swede Carlson controlled his breathing and vocal apparatus deliberately. "Where is it now, Janey?" he asked.

"In my bag." She felt down in the seat beside her. "At least it was there. I haven't taken it out." She moved her slim hips and felt down on the other side of her by the window. "Oh—I didn't bring my bag. I must have . . . When I got up, back there, I must have left it, or it dropped on the floor. That's what I must have done. It was in my lap when Buck came and said . . . said Gus wanted me."

Carlson reached for the door handle. He let it go and turned again on the front seat.

"You two go back now," he said quietly. "You get your bag, Janey. If you can do it, don't let anybody see you're interested in it at all, hear? If it's there, I want it and I want it quick. You bring it out, Gus."

"And if it's not there?"

"If it's not there," Swede Carlson said quietly, "I'll be mighty gaw-dam interested—but I won't be surprised. It's gettin' to be somebody else's turn to be surprised."

TWENTY

"—AND YOU TWO go in there actin' like you're speakin', whether you are or not. I don't want this gummed up, now." Swede Carlson spoke brusquely and meant it when Janey pulled away from Gus trying to help her out of the car and started off ahead of him.

She stopped and waited, not wooden but taut and very much alive. He took her arm again.

"Janey—please! For God's sake, Janey . . ."

She wrenched away. "Stop it!" she said hotly. "I've told you I don't care anything about any of you any more. You or Connie or anybody else. And you might just as well hear the rest of it. I've spent all the money we ever had. I threw it all away—the whole thousand dollars. I blew it in on the slot machines. It's all gone. There's three dollars and forty-two cents left in the bank. Fergie told me so this afternoon. So leave me alone, do you hear me? You can go back to Connie. You're always leaving me to go with Orvie, so you can go with Connie and I'll just go with Orvie! I guess he'll still be willing to marry me and if he isn't I'll find somebody else."

They were almost at the end of the asphalt drive of the Club house walk. Janey went ahead of him onto the brick. "Hello, Fergie," she said sweetly. "You're not going home this early, are you?"

Gus came miserably on behind her. "Shoving off, Fergie?"

"Yes," Jim Ferguson said. He held the door open for Janey. "Martha's staying, but I'm going along. I'm going duck shooting with my son in the morning, so I thought I'd better turn in early. I wouldn't want him to see me miss too many. And Martha won't let me take any dog hair along when I've got a gun and the kids. So long, you two."

Gus looked after him as he closed the door. Wretched as he was, he still knew a lot of words when he heard them. So Fergie was going duck shooting. Ordinarily, he'd have said so and shut up. But everybody was wacky tonight. Even John Maynard. He was over at the cloakroom getting his overcoat and hat. Uncle Nelly was with him. They weren't what you would call vocal. Miss Nelly had had too much to drink and John Maynard not enough.

"Sorry about your accident, Gus," Maynard said briefly. "I want to talk to you on Monday."

"Okay," Gus said. He added to himself, "—And if I'm fired I've already quit."

He followed Janey up the companionway. She stopped halfway along and waited for him, her blue eyes looking through him, not at him, just the way they had in the pantry that morning, when he'd first learned Janey was not all sweet and warm and putty in anybody's hands.

"Poor Uncle Nelly," she said. She let her hand rest lightly in Gus's crooked arm. "It *is* ulcers. He told me. They're all popped again and he feels dreadful. He's quit playing the slot machines too.—Hello! Hello, there!" She smiled at some people Gus didn't know, coming out of the bar. "Do come back to Smithville, won't you? I hope you have a good trip."

At the door of the bar she turned and looked into the mirror. "Oh, wait a minute, will you, Gus? Or why don't you get a drink while I powder my nose? My bag's over there."

She went on into the room. "Hello, Janey! Hi there, Janey!" It started all over again . . . Janey back once more from a year in the bush. She smiled at everybody and went over to her table. Orvie Rogers was still there waiting. Orvie and Connie. Martha Ferguson and Dorsey Syms were at the slot machines again.

"Did I leave my bag here? I need my lipstick."

"I don't see it," Orvie said.

"Where's Gus?"

"He's getting a drink, Connie. I guess he needs one. He'll be over in a second. Why don't you wait for him? He's in a foul mood."

Orvie was looking for the bag. Gus saw him search around on the seat and dive under the table. He came up with it in one hand, brushing it off with the other.

"Somebody's walked all over it, Janey." He handed it to her. "I guess you dropped it."

"No wonder," Connie Maynard said. "Gus barging in—"

Janey turned away. "I'll be right back, Orvie. Order me something, will you?"

She went past Gus at the bar and across the hall to the powder room. He saw her close the door, and moved out with his drink to meet her. People were coming in and out. He could go over and look at the pictures of last June's races on the wall opposite the powder-room door without being too obvious about it. And almost at once she was there by his elbow again. He looked down at her. She shook her head. A roar came out of the bar as some one got a jack pot. She raised herself on tiptoes as she slid something wrapped in white cleansing tissue into his pocket.

"It's gone."

She spoke quickly under the covering racket from the bar.

"Give that to Swede. It's my compact. It's got powder on it and he must have touched it, fishing around. He couldn't have had gloves on tonight. Be careful of it."

She pointed to the picture on the wall. "That's a lovely thing. Just look at Orvie's boat. It's beautiful, isn't it?"

She smiled at some people coming up the stairs. "And I think you ought to change that dressing, Gus. It looks awful. There's a kit in the cloakroom. Do you want Connie to come down and help you? She's had first-aid, before the war. Or during it, which was it? The last war, I mean."

She smiled at him and joined some of her friends heading back to the bar. "No, thanks, I've got a drink waiting for me."

He stood staring stupidly at the picture of Orvie's sailing craft. Compact . . . fingerprints . . . That was fast thinking in the clutch. He'd never have thought of it. How had Janey got so smart all of a sudden? Or had Janey always been smart while one Gus Blake was always being dumb?

It was still in his mind when he came back up from giving the compact to Swede Carlson—still there, and heavily underlined. Swede hadn't been surprised that Janey had used her head. He'd also taken time out to do the underlining by telling about the footprint in the back yard that Janey had found and the kid had planted grass seed on top of . . . that Gus Blake had in fact told the kid to plant it on, though he was already too cut down to size to tell Carlson that and Janey evidently hadn't. And Swede Carlson was in a hurry too. The lucky piece could have been Wernitz's. Janey's father might know. The little gambler could have told his only friend, on one of those long moonlit nights. Lieutenant Williams of the City Police was on his way to the Rogers plant, Carlson was following. Two birds with one missing lucky piece.

Gus ordered his second milk punch. The first had helped. He didn't feel as groggy as he had. The milk was as useful on his empty stomach as the fine fattening bourbon that laced it. And two would be plenty; he had to keep his wits about him till Swede got back. He looked about. The only people left there who'd been at the Maynards' were Orvie and Dorsey over at the table with Connie and Janey, except Al Reed, who'd won the jackpot and was breaking his neck to put it all back again. But he'd come up the stairs when Gus and Janey came back from Swede's car, before Janey retrieved her bag. He tried to remember who else had been in the room when he took Janey out the first time. The only people he could think of were the ones at the table with her now. There could

have been others in the reading room across the hall, or somebody at
the slot machines. It would have to be somebody who could have seen
Janey go out without her bag and who could move over to the table and
join the rest of them on perfectly casual terms. And while any of the
Maynards' friends could do that, this had to be one of a particular
group of the Maynards' friends.

He realized suddenly that going along by tortuous and unwilling
stages to exactly what it meant, he was unconsciously balking at every
step of the way. It was full of complicating negatives obscuring a final
conclusion. If it was not somebody he'd not seen who came to the table,
it had to be someone who was there when he pulled Janey away. If it
had to be somebody who was at the Maynards' party who had to risk his
neck to look in the velvet bag she'd had at the party and had with her
now, it had to be one of the people who made up his and Janey's most
intimate circle of friends. It had to be Orvie Rogers, or Dorsey, Uncle
Nelly Syms, or John Maynard, or Jim Ferguson. They were the only ones
at the table when Buck took his message over to Janey. No one of them
would have broken into his house.

He was face to face with it finally.—No one of them would have
killed Doc Wernitz. That was cockeyed. It was not anything anybody,
namely Gus Blake, could bring himself then if ever to believe. He
downed his milk punch. He was sweating, first cold then hot. It must be
his accident catching up with him. Or the milk. Milk was dangerous
stuff. He ordered another drink of it. Plain milk, or was it plain bourbon,
this time, and tried to get his mind around to where it was working
straight.

"What's the matter, Gus? Come on over."

Connie Maynard's voice came across the room. Her cheeks were
flushed and her eyes bright. Connie had been lapping it up, and Connie
when she was getting high could also get definitely unpleasant, if people
didn't do what she wanted them to. He could see symptoms in the yellow-green cat's eyes now. She tossed a ten-dollar bill to her cousin
Dorsey.

"Play it for me, Dorse. We'll go halves on it, and don't hold out on
me, dear. Bring me a drink, Gus. Scotch."

She turned back to the table. "Why don't you kids go dance?" She
looked from Orvie to Janey. "Go on. I want to talk to Gus. Business,
dear. Newspaper business, I mean."

Bringing her drink, Gus saw Orvie look at Janey and the two of them get up, and Janey, smart little girl, slip her bag off her wrist and leave it casually on the seat. She moved out with Orvie just as Connie Maynard got herself started.

"Gus . . . I'm going to get Dad to give me the paper," she said abruptly. "How'd you like that? Then we wouldn't have to worry about what people liked and what they didn't like."

"That's fine," Gus said. He slipped over behind the table. "I've decided to quit anyway. Monday? How'll that be?"

She straightened up slowly. "What do you mean, you've decided to quit?" Her eyes smouldered.

Gus saw Janey stop for an instant. She didn't look around. He raised his voice.

"Just that," he said. "If Janey's sore at me there's no use my sticking around Smithville. Corny as it sounds, it's that old woman-I-love stuff. And I wouldn't work for a dame anyway, Con."

He saw Janey's body stiffen before she took hold of Orvie's arm and the two of them went on through the arch and around to where the orchestra was playing on the enclosed deck. He leaned back and raised his glass. Connie leaned forward, her lips tight and her eyes narrowed.

"Cut it out, Connie." He shook his head at Martha Ferguson and Dorsey, easing in to help him out. If they got in it, the barmen would have to call the cops. Martha's red hair and the martinis she was still drinking after dinner didn't mix into any smooth blend, and Dorsey was always cockier the higher he got.

He grinned at them. "This fight's private. You two keep out. Go play the slot machines. Here's five bucks, Martha." He took a bill out of his pocket and tossed it to her. "Play it for me. In the nickel machine—it'll last longer. Go away, both of you. Connie and I are talking business."

While Martha Ferguson hesitated there was a scream from in front of the fifty-cent machine. They were both off to see who'd won.

"—What do you mean, you won't work for a dame?" Connie Maynard demanded angrily. She was still leaning forward over the table, her eyes shooting sparks. "If Dad gives me the paper, you've got a contract, haven't you?"

"I said cut it out, Connie," Gus repeated deliberately. "Let's get this straight; sweetie . . . and it's tonight and last night, or this morning, whatever you want to call it, that I'm talking about at the same time. It's no soap, Con. Just relax. Nobody warms up last year's cold mutton. You or me. Especially you, Con. You know it as well as I do."

They were alone in the corner. Everybody concerned was giving them all the room they needed, and the slot machines for once in their metallic life span were co-operating. They were paying off all over the place. When that happened, murder, arson and mayhem could go on behind them with no one to care or even see.

"Look, Connie. You could have married me if you'd wanted to. You didn't. It was a damned good thing for both of us. We'd have fought like a couple of polecats, and if we hadn't murdered each other first we'd have been washed up a long time before now. You know it, and I know it. So let's skip it. You don't love me and I don't love you. That's daid, honey, daid and buried. It's—"

Across the room at the bar, Buck was holding his arm up, signaling elaborately. Gus stopped.

"Miss Maynard! Mr. Maynard wants her at the telephone."

Connie straightened up. The flush on her white face had long since darkened into a congested purple. She looked slowly around.

"Go talk to your father on the phone," Gus said. He started to move around to help her to her feet. She was in no need of help. She rose in a single co-ordinated flash, put one hand on the table and leaned across it. Her other hand came up and out before Gus could move. It caught him in a stinging blow on the side of the face, the metal of her big ring gashing his cheek that had escaped the wreck.

He sat quietly, his eyes colder than the blazing blue sapphire in the ring. He didn't want to look around. The people at the slot machines wouldn't have noticed, but the men at the bar couldn't fail to.

"You won't work for a dame . . ." Her voice was soft and malignant as sin. "We'll see. I'll ask my father right now. We'll see what you'll do."

She turned and went across the floor, her head high.

Gus ran his tongue around his lips and raised his glass. He looked over at the people in the room. If any one had seen what had happened, they were all too polite or too scared to show it. The barmen especially. They were all busy as hell getting bottles out from under the bar. All he could see was broad white backs. And coming cheerfully in then he saw Orvie Rogers.

TWENTY-ONE

ORVIE picked himself up a drink at the bar and brought it over.

"Saw Connie. She's mad as hell." He slipped into the seat beside Gus. "I feel sorry for the poor devil that marries her."

"Where's Janey?" Gus asked curtly.

"Oh, somebody grabbed her. That's the trouble. You dance three steps with Janey and there's a stag line you didn't even see. But I guess you're used to that too." He took a drink and put his glass down. "As a matter of fact," he said solemnly, "I wanted to talk to you, Gus."

"Oh, God," Gus thought. Was this going to be on a high and noble plane? Was Orvie going to put everything on the up and up? I'm going to marry your wife, old fellow, but no hard feelings, what? For a minute he thought the milk and bourbon were neither of them staying down.

"You don't mind, do you, Gus?"

"No, no," Gus said. "Not at all. Go ahead, Orvie. What's on your mind?"

"It's about Janey, chiefly," Orvie Rogers said.

Gus closed his eyes and tightened his grip on his glass and on himself. Connie had socked him. If he let Orvie have one, it would be a record night even for the Sailing Club. He opened his eyes and cleared his throat.

"What about Janey, Orvie?"

"Why—" Orvie stopped and glanced quickly around the room. "First let me give you a tip on something else. Don't for God's sake tell anybody I told you." He leaned forward and lowered his voice. "Don't let Connie kid you about her old man giving her the paper. He doesn't even own it."

Gus stared at him. The pale eyes under the blond hair were regarding him with owlish earnestness. He straightened up slowly.

"What are you—"

"Ssssh." Orvie looked nervously about again. "That's right, Gus. Dad told me today. Maynard hardly owns anything around here, Gus. Dad told me today." He lowered his voice still more. "Maynard's just a front guy, on a lot of things he's supposed to own—like the paper, and his bank stock too. Not that he hasn't stashed away a lot of what he made being a front guy.—You know who owns the paper, or did own it?"

Gus shook his head, still staring at him.

"Wernitz," said Orvie Rogers. "Doc Wernitz. Vanaman—he's a lawyer here Wernitz hired to keep his eye on Maynard, and I guess he had another one to keep his eye on him—Vanaman called Dad from New York this morning and told him Maynard better not sell any of his bank stock on the quiet. It really was Wernitz's. Dad was sore as hell, because he didn't want any gambling dough in his bank. I wish you'd seen him. Anyway, Vanaman told him Wernitz owned most of the paper. Maynard owns ten per cent. So you don't have to worry about . . . anything."

Gus sat there quietly. It was one of the things a guy learned in the reporting business, and he'd had a rough refresher course from Swede Carlson in the last couple of hours.

"How long has Wernitz owned the paper?" he asked calmly.

"About five years. He was the one figured it'd make some dough if they got the right guy to run it. Isn't that why they got you?"

Gus raised his glass to his lips and choked, coughing, as he put it down. They'd got him cheap, too. Cheaper than he'd thought. He grinned sardonically, thinking about his deal with Maynard, all friendly and informal. It wasn't sixty per cent of all the stock. It was sixty per cent of Maynard's stock. Who owned all the stock had been clearly understood, by both of them—in different ways. He could see it all down in black and white. Maynard wasn't to sell any of it for the next four years. That was the deal, and it had nothing to say about what he'd already sold. He raised his glass and was able to swallow straight this time.

"Well, I just thought I'd tell you," Orvie said. "Janey was pretty upset when she heard Connie. Now about Janey, Gus . . ."

"Yeah," Gus said. He pulled himself together. "What about Janey?" If he could take Wernitz's owning the paper he could take anything. So, let's have it . . .

"Why, it's about this." Orvie pulled an envelope part way out of his pocket and stuck it back again. "I mean, this is why I came by your house this morning. You know I'm crazy about Janey. She's swell. But I don't need to tell you that."

He blinked solemnly into his glass. "It's just that I wouldn't want you to get any funny ideas. I thought you were sore this morning, and I wouldn't blame you. But I just came by because . . . why, because Dad wanted to send Janey a check."

Gus looked at him through a bewildered fog.

"You see, Janey was sore because you and Con were so busy all the time," Orvie said. "Not that it's my business," he added hastily. "All I mean is . . ." He stopped, looking at Gus earnestly. "I always seem to do the wrong thing, but I'm sure this . . . it isn't wrong to tell you this, Gus.—You see, Janey was sore about you and Connie, and she was hitting the slot machines. Nobody could stop her. You know. So she was overdrawn at the bank. Doc Wernitz collected checks the way some guys do stamps, and he dumped 'em all in yesterday. Fergie didn't want to embarrass Janey, or you, I guess, so he told Dad and John Maynard. And you know Dad. He's crazy about Janey, and her old man—both of 'em—so he sent me in with this."

Orvie touched his pocket. "—To give to Janey to cover her overdraft."

Gus waited.

"But Janey wouldn't take it," Orvie went on quickly. "She called Fergie. He was at the bank all afternoon. And she says he told her she didn't have an overdraft."

His solemn face broke into a happy grin. He put his head down on his hands then and laughed like a crazy fool.

Gus watched him silently as long as he could.

"This is supposed to be funny, some way, Orvie?"

"It sure is," Orvie said cheerfully. He controlled his mirth with an effort. "At least, I think it is. I think it's funny as hell. Because she's right. She hasn't got an overdraft. Only Dad didn't know it, and I thought I'd better not tell him. He's funny about dough, you know."

He looked quickly around the room again.

"—Maynard took the checks home with him. I don't know why. He's not supposed to, even if he is a director. Dad didn't know it and he wouldn't like it. You know, hanky-panky in the bank sort of stuff. But when Maynard took 'em out, he had to cover 'em with his own check. And this is the pay-off. I don't know what Maynard was going to do with 'em, but it was something Mrs. Maynard didn't like—or thought she wasn't going to like. She didn't even know they were checks. All she knew was there was something in the library desk drawer that Maynard and Connie had been talking about. She had me stand guard, and she opened the drawer. She found Janey's checks with 'NO FUNDS' on 'em.''

He looked at Gus earnestly. "You know what she did? She put 'em in the fire."

He rocked with mirth again. "So Janey doesn't have an overdraft. Maybe you don't think it's funny, but I do. I think John Maynard getting soaked three hundred and twenty bucks is funny as hell."

His face sobered and he looked at Gus with owlish earnestness. Gus sat there a minute without saying anything. "Orvie," he said then, "I guess you've got something, at that."

"Well, I just thought I'd tell you." He pushed aside his glass. "I've got to go rescue Janey from some of those goons with web feet." He started off and stopped, a sheepish smile on his face. "Maybe I shouldn't tell you, and don't get sore, Gus, but it was Janey sent me in here. I was supposed to get rid of Connie. Janey's changed her mind, Gus, about this to hell with you and Connie can have you line she's been talking. I knew she didn't mean it. You know what women are like. But she heard you and Connie. She says if you're going to quit you'll have to take her and little Jane with you, and if Connie gets the paper you'll quit anyway. She says Connie'll be the kind of a boss you could take about two days. So I didn't tell her about the Wernitz deal. Men ought to sort of stick together. I—"

Gus put his hand up to his revolving head and held it there a moment. He put it down, got to his feet, and held it out. He shook Orvie's hand. "Orvie," he said, "you're dead right. God help us if we don't." He took a deep breath of the stale-grain-and-neutral-spirits air of the Sailing Club and looked at Orvie with fresher and less leaden-weighted gray eyes. "Orvie," he said, "—Orvie, I'd like to buy you a drink."

Orvie Rogers' solemn face lighted up. "Oh, thanks, Gus! Thanks a lot!" He glanced at his watch. Then he glanced at the door. "Why, thanks just the same, Gus," he said briskly, "but some other time, I guess. I . . . I see Miss Maynard returning, and count me out. I'm going to get Janey. Now she's not so upset and everything, I guess she can take Connie on better than I can." He raised his voice. "Well, sure swell having a chance to talk to you, Gus." He turned back, lowering his voice again. "—You're not sore, about all this stuff . . ."

"Not at all, Orvie. Not at all."

He'd said it to Orvie once before that day. It sounded different this time, both to him and Orvie.

Connie Maynard came swiftly across the room. "Go away, Orvie," she said. Her voice sounded as if some one was tightening an invisible necklace around her throat.

"Just going, Con," Orvie said cheerfully. The glance he gave Gus over the top of her tawny head added, "You're telling *me*."

"Gus!" She put her hand on his arm. "Gus!"

"Keep away from me, lady." He dropped his arm and moved back. Something had happened to her. The purple blotches in her cheeks were gone, and the yellow brimstone.

"Gus, I'm sorry! I'm terribly sorry! I didn't mean it, about the paper, or—"

"You mean your dad just told you?" Gus inquired easily. "That he doesn't own the paper?"

She caught her breath and steadied herself. Her fingers pressed hard on the table. "What . . . how did you know?" she demanded sharply. "Who—"

"Never mind. It's my job to know these things." It sounded good, at least. "But I'm still quitting, if that's what's eating you. I'm particular who I work for."

Looking at her, he saw something was wrong beyond what she was saying. She wasn't listening to him. Her eyes were moving frantically from side to side. She was waiting desperately for him to shut up. There was no use going on anyway. It was a little hard to explain even to himself, how he could have gone on working for slot-machine dough without knowing it or being coerced by it in any way and get so almighty righteous all of a sudden, without even knowing what was going to happen now the local king of the slots was dead and couldn't take it with him. He stopped and let her have a chance. She took it breathlessly.

"I've said I'm sorry. But that's not the trouble. Oh, please, Gus! This is on the level. I'm asking you to help me out. Just once, Gus. Something's happened at home."

He pulled himself sharply to attention. His own personal mixup and the handsome roseate dawn of hope that had taken over and dissolved the nightmare of writhing despair inside him, since Orvie's bumbling confidence, had pretty well anæsthetized him to the real purpose of his being there at the Club. And Connie wasn't being funny.

"What—"

"I don't know," she said quickly. "I . . . I'm afraid it's Uncle Nelly. I don't know whether he's sick or . . . or what. Dad wouldn't say. All he said was for me not to say anything to Aunt Mamie or Martha or anybody but to get Dorsey to come and help do something. And Dorsey's tight. Look at him over there. I tried to give him the high sign from the door but he won't pay any attention to me. I don't want to tell him. One Maynard scene tonight is all the Club could take. I'm sorry, Gus . . . but please help me out."

He looked up. Janey had come back with Orvie and was watching them. She couldn't have helped hearing Connie's last few words. It was a risk he couldn't take. Orvie might think he knew what women were like, but he'd be damned if Gus Blake did. Janey might easily change her mind another time and leave him in a thicker, hotter soup than the one he'd just crawled out of.

He shook his head. "Sorry, Con. You'll have to get Dorsey home yourself."

"—That's mean, Gus." He winced. It was Janey who said it. She came on the few steps to the table, her blue eyes soft and quite serious. Or apparently. He was no longer sure of anything about this girl Janey. "Go on with her, Gus," she said earnestly. "Orvie and I'll stay and dance. We'll keep Martha here with us."

Connie stiffened. It was bitter fruit to take from Janey's hand. She took it. "Thanks," she said curtly. As she walked away Gus looked apprehensively at Janey. She nodded almost imperceptibly and moved in behind the table. "Martha!" she called. "Come on over and talk to me and Orvie. We've got a wonderful idea." She gave Orvie an amused smile as he moved in beside her. "—Think of one, quick."

Gus followed Connie over to the machines.

"Come on, Dorse." She waited for Gus to move in beside her. "Gus and I are going over to Tony Modesto's." She thought desperately of some place he might be willing to go to until they could get him outside and tell him about Uncle Nelly. She didn't want him to go into a crying jag there in the Club. "Come on, sweetie. Janey'll let Gus go if we've got a chaperon. Tony's got kale for fifteen cents a bunch and he'll give Gus tomorrow's dope."

"Don't play the horses," Dorsey said amiably. His voice was a little thick. "That's Dad. And I just got three bells."

He put another dime in the machine. "This thing's hot tonight. Or Martha just dropped twenty-three bucks in it, so it ought to be."

"Come on, Dorsey," Gus said easily. "The jackpot'll be ready by the time we get back."

Dorsey pulled the handle. The three plums came. "Oh, boy!" he said. He picked up his fourteen dimes and put another in.

"Come on, Dorsey."

He turned and looked at Gus, and seemed to realize something was going on. "Okay." He followed them to the door. "It's not . . . There's nothing wrong? Dad isn't sick, is he? He looked like hell tonight."

"I don't know, Dorsey. We've got to get out home."

They got their coats in the cloakroom in the foyer and went out, Dorsey staggering a little as the cold fresh air hit him.

"Wondered why Uncle John was taking him home so early. Where is he?"

"At our house," Connie repeated. "Open the window, Dorsey, and breathe. You've got to sober up before we get there."

She was entirely sober herself. The crack on the side of his face had probably done a third of it, Gus thought, her conversation with John Maynard the rest. She drove now as if she'd been a white-ribbon girl all her life. There were two other cars in the drive in front of the white-pillared porch. Connie's hands were cold as she switched off the engine. If Uncle Nelly was really sick, they'd have taken him to the hospital, not here. It was something else. Aunt Mamie . . . ?

She slid across the seat after the two men and waited until Gus slammed the car door. Nobody but the family knew how much Aunt Mamie depended on the weedy unobtrusive prop that Uncle Nelly was. . . . Inside the door, she stopped and listened. She ran across and opened the library door, Dorsey behind her, Gus behind him.

"Oh," she said. She stopped short.

"Come in, both of you," John Maynard said.

His jaw tightened as he saw Gus. "You better come in too, now you're here, Blake."

Gus looked through the open door at Uncle Nelly. He was sick, but he was at least still alive. He sat huddled in the leather armchair by the desk, as green almost as the leather itself. His eyes were fixed on the floor, his long bloodless fingers kneading his forehead.

"—We've got a little serious business that don't get into the paper, Gus," John Maynard said quietly. "Come in and shut the door."

TWENTY-TWO

GUS BLAKE shut the door behind him, and started a little in spite of himself. John Maynard and Uncle Nelly were not the only ones there. In the place of honor at John Maynard's desk sat Orvie Rogers' father, his brows beetling, his face set. His dead-fish eyes were fixed on the guy who was going to turn in early to take his son duck shooting at daybreak. Jim Ferguson looked as if he was about to turn in deeper and longer than he'd said.

"—Dad!" Dorsey Syms went forward quickly toward his father, his face pale and alarmed. As his eyes fell on the man who had been sitting on the sofa facing John Maynard in front of the fireplace he came to a sudden stop. Mr. Hugo Vanaman took a step nearer the desk and Nathan Rogers. Gus's eyes followed Dorsey's as they moved around the room. He stared for an instant at Williams of the City Police and Carlson of the County Constabulary standing by the curtained windows, together and yet somehow curiously apart from the others. Dorsey Syms turned back, his eyes moving from one of them to the other, fixed in turn on each one of them, the sick-faced men and the grim-faced men. He took another step toward his father.

"Dad, are you— What is this? What's going on here?"

The eyes of every man in the room except his father rested on him. Uncle Nelly was staring in sick helplessness down at the floor.

John Maynard said softly, "It's all up, Dorsey."

Dorsey swung round to him. "—What do you mean?"

"Just that. It's all up. You're goin' to be put under arrest, Dorsey. These men—"

Dorsey Syms stared at him. "What do you mean, I'm going to be put under arrest?" he asked coolly. His easy smile came to his lips. The Maynard smile, Gus Blake thought. The Maynard charm. The Maynard confidence. Dorsey looked around the room. He swayed a little. The cold air had sobered him up some, Gus thought. Not enough, perhaps. Always cocky when he was tight.

"Under *arrest?*" Dorsey repeated. His voice had a shade of good-natured irony. "Don't be silly. You're joking, aren't you? There's such a thing as proof, you know. You can't prove a gawdam thing on me, you and your flatfoots, and don't fool yourselves I don't know it. I was at the races. I was nowhere near the Wernitz house last night."

There was silence in the room, heavy, cold, deadly, filling every part and corner, enduring. It prolonged, dragged on inexorably, unbearably, it seemed to Gus Blake, second after second. It was as if some giant steel coil, wound to its last possible turn, had met and absorbed another and held tight, no one daring to move or breathe for fear the monster would burst loose, shattering itself and them. The silence held, seemed to gather, swelling, with some kind of quality of shock, of stupefaction, expanding as if it would burst the room itself. Gus looked at Swede Carlson. His face was not expressionless now as he stared silently at Dorsey, his jaw sagging a little, his colorless eyes slowly lighting. It came to Gus then in an instantaneous blinding flash. The Wernitz murder had nothing to do with why these men were here. It was not the Wernitz murder they were arresting him for. And Dorsey Syms didn't realize it. He stood there handsome and arrogant, swaying a little, almost erect, smiling his pleasant smile, any surprise concealed, cocky as a teen-age goon swaggering down an alley in the slums.

"This is just crazy," Dorsey Syms said. His voice was easy and courteous. "You gentlemen can't be serious about this. Even supposing I'd done it . . . let's be realistic. No jury'd take a Filipino slot-machine mechanic's word against mine—if that could be what you're banking on. You haven't got an atom of proof. I wasn't anywhere near the Wernitz place. But . . . even that lucky piece you were all groping for. You couldn't prove it belonged to . . . anybody in particular. And you couldn't prove I ever touched it, even if it did belong to anybody in particular. You—"

Swede Carlson came out from the windows.

"Now you sort of foolishly bring the matter up, Syms," he said, "I sort of guess I can. And I can prove a lot more."

He took a handful of white cleansing tissue out of his pocket and laid it on the table. He unfolded it. A metal powder container glittered softly in the light.

"This is Janey Blake's compact. It was in her bag at the Sailing Club tonight when you were sitting beside her on the bench. You saw it slip out of her lap when she got up to go out with Gus. You got the lucky piece out and dropped the bag on the floor again so nobody could see you. This compact's got prints on it that aren't Janey Blake's, Syms."

Dorsey laughed. "Nuts," he said. "Nuts to you, Carlson. I saw a bag there. I opened it to see whose it was."

"And dropped it on the floor under the table?"

"It must have got knocked off the seat."

His eyes moved from face to face.

"And I've got another print to show you." Carlson turned and nodded to Williams.

Dorsey's smile was still easy. "Do people go around leaving finger-prints these days? I thought every fool knew enough to—"

"This ain't a fingerprint."

Carlson unwrapped the object Lieutenant Williams handed him.

"This is a footprint, Syms. It's made from a cast of a footprint you made—in the Blakes' back yard, when you went over there at night to get the lucky piece you knew you had to get, that you took out at Wernitz's and put in the slot machine here by mistake. That's what Williams and I came here for, startin' to find a shoe that'll fit this."

"That lucky piece doesn't mean a thing, Carlson. You don't know where it came from, anything about—"

"That's where you're wrong again, Syms. It came right from Doc Wernitz. It's been described to us by a friend of Wernitz's who knew about it and's seen it. Janey Blake's father, Syms. That's somethin' you overlooked too. You figured because that Filipino boy you slugged still can't tell us anythin' about it we couldn't find out about it. But you knew it could be a dead giveaway. That's why you had to get it back. That's what you were doin' when you made this footprint here, in the Blake's back yard. Looks mighty like the shape of your foot, Syms. You mind takin' off your right shoe?"

Dorsey Sym's face was suddenly as gray as ashes. Swede Carlson looked at him curiously.

"It couldn't be you're such a conceited, arrogant so-and-so," he asked slowly, "that you still got it on you? And by God, that's where it is? Take that right shoe off, Syms."

"The hell I will." His voice was thicker. "I've got rights. This is absurd. I—"

The elder Rogers spoke, his voice steely. "Take that shoe off, Syms."

Dorsey hesitated. He raised his right foot and reached down to it. Carlson took a quick step forward. He caught Dorsey's hand, caught his foot, took the shoe carefully off. He held it out at arm's length, turned away from Dorsey toward the others and turned the shoe slowly over.

There was a bright small flash, a soft thud as a small object hit the carpet. It rolled and was still. Swede Carlson bent down and picked it up. He held it in the palm of his hand.

"—You got anythin' else to say, Syms?"

"Yes." His face was white now. "This is . . . I didn't even know Wernitz. I haven't any motive . . . you've got to prove—"

Gus jerked his head around as John Maynard spoke in his deliberate drawl.

"You've talked too much already, Dorsey. Ain't much more for you to say. I reckon your motive couldn't be much clearer. I told you when you came in it was all up. You misunderstood me, Dorsey."

"What do you mean, I—"

"We didn't know nothin' about you and Wernitz when you came in this room. We got you here for somethin' entirely different, Dorsey."

The ashy-gray of Dorsey's face turned slowly white as he stared at his uncle, speechless for an instant. He found his voice. "I . . . don't know what you're—"

"I expect you'll know when I tell you Miss Mattie Lewis died of a heart attack at nine o'clock last night."

Gus Blake's eyes moved from one to the other of them. The sweat stood out on Dorsey's forehead, glistening in the lamplight. His lips moved, repeating the name soundlessly.

"That's right. Miss Mattie Lewis. And because Gus Blake took the day off, your cousin Connie put the announcement of her death and her obituary over on the want-ad page instead of the front page where it belonged. You didn't see it. If you'd seen it, you could have rushed around and saved yourself again. Happens her nephew has to go out of town tomorrow, and he brought her savings book round to Ferguson this afternoon. Miss Mattie deposited $1,200 Thursday. It's credited in her book, bringin' her total to $9,380. In the bank records she's credited with $120 deposit, Thursday, and a total of $3,380. Wernitz's savings book's disappeared, Dorsey. Vanaman can't find it in his safe and the police didn't find it on his body. But Wernitz kept Vanaman informed of his accounts. He says his total is $8,240. The bank records show him at $4,240. That's what we called you in here to explain. How many accounts you've been jugglin' the last five years we don't know yet, but Ferguson's callin' all the savings deposit books in."

Dorsey Syms moved his hands slowly down the sides of his coat, wiping the cold sweat off his palms.

"You thought Wernitz was closin' his account and you didn't have the four thousand to pay out. There wasn't time, Friday afternoon when you heard he was leavin', to rig it so you'd be in the clear. And Miss Mattie dyin' suddenly leaves you in the same spot, Dorsey. Only if it hadn't been for that, God knows how long before we'd have caught up with you. Mr. Rogers thought the police ought to be here when we asked you to explain if you could, and that's the only reason they were here in this room. And I wish you'd get this man out of my house, Carlson."

TWENTY-THREE

CONNIE MAYNARD sat huddled in a corner of the sofa, staring blindly into the empty fireplace. Gus Blake stood there, one elbow on the mantel. There was an incredible and ironic quality about it that left him still working back through it from the beginning, trying to make out how it could have happened the way it did. They were alone in the house. Jim Ferguson and Orvie's father had gone. The Maynards had gone to take poor old Uncle Nelly home, to help him cushion the shock for Aunt Mamie, if it could be cushioned. Of all of them Mr. Rogers was the one who could take it easiest. Dorsey had never been a friend of his, and to him right was right, wrong was wrong, and in a bank integrity added up to the biggest asset of all.

"I ought to have noticed something was up when they all showed at the Club and all left," Gus thought. If none of them had showed, people might have begun to wonder a little. He got out a cigarette. So the captains and the kings were gone, and he and Connie were the only ones left. He thought of Mr. Hugo Vanaman for an instant, who had eased out without any one's being aware of him. It could have been a great moment for Mr. Vanaman, seeing what he called very high-class people having to turn on one of their own.

Connie reached out to the cigarette box on the table, and left her hand there, still staring into the fireplace.

"Dorsey always was a heel," she said abruptly. "I never thought he was that big a heel. Oh, it's awful, Gus! He . . . he had everything—family, education. If he wanted money, why didn't he work for it? Dad and Mr. Rogers both offered him jobs he'd have made a lot more money in . . ."

She stopped for an instant. "Made it honestly. And he's got plenty of brain—"

She broke off without finishing the word. Brains. Who was she to talk about brains? She closed her eyes wearily. Who am I to talk about anything? she thought suddenly. Pride, arrogance, conceit . . . all the things everybody could see in Dorsey, her father had described to her in herself that same afternoon. Cocksure, conceited, thought everybody else was stupid. She'd thought the same thing. Even after John Maynard had given her the going-over he had, she'd gone on being cocksure and conceited, until Swede Carlson had caught her out down there in the play room. What if he knew what she'd really done? She caught her breath. What if Janey had taken the capsules and had never waked up? How different would she be from Dorsey now? But she wasn't a thief.

She moved uncomfortably on the sofa. She was a thief. A different kind, maybe a worse kind. She closed her eyes again to keep from seeing Gus at the end of the hearth. She hadn't got away with it . . . but neither had Dorsey. They were both too arrogant, too conceited. Or maybe people didn't get away with things as easily as they thought. Maybe that was what her father had meant. Maybe he'd just been giving her a chance, trying her out to see what kind of stuff she had in her. What if he came back thinking she was really just another Dorsey, different in degree but not in kind? She put down the lighter and threw her cigarrette into the ashes in the fireplace.

"Take it easy, Con," Gus said.

"I can't." She got to her feet. "I can't take it easy. I'm just like Dorsey. I'm the same sort of heel he is, Gus."

He looked around at her.

"It's true, Gus. I'm as rotten in my way as Dorsey is in his." She said it passionately. "You don't know what a terrible thing I did. I saw Janey take some—"

"Stop it, Connie. Just shut up. Janey told us. It didn't take much to figure something was the matter with you last night. Carlson figured it and so did I. It doesn't matter now. Janey's Janey. You can't beat Janey. And if you'd learn what you are, maybe you'd pull up your socks and quit being a stinking witch. I told you that tonight. All this business ought to make you start playing the game, instead of trying to beat it, the way both you and Dorsey've been doing."

She looked steadily at him, her face colorless, her eyes wide.

"And don't come over and give me another crack. I wouldn't take it again."

"Oh, no, Gus. That . . . that's not what I was thinking." She moved back to the sofa unsteadily. "You say things to yourself, and even say them out loud, but you don't really believe them. You can forget them. If somebody else says them, that means they know them too. You can't forget that so easily." She moistened her lips and put her hands up to her forehead. "Gus . . . if you and Janey will ever have anything to do with me any more . . . I mean, if you see me starting to act like . . . like myself, I guess I mean, will you stop me? If you don't—"

"Will do," Gus said.

A cheerful voice sounded out in the hall. "Hey? What goes on?" Connie sprang to her feet. Orvie was out there. Gus moved toward the door. Janey must be with him. And they hadn't heard yet.

"Don't! Don't tell them, Gus. Later. Let's tell them later." She whispered it desperately under the covering sound of the front door slamming shut and their voices outside.

Gus nodded. "Hi, there! Come on in."

They came in, Orvie and Janey, their cheeks wind-flushed, Janey's tow-hair blown out from the black velvet bow on the top of her head.

"How's Uncle Nelly?" she asked quickly, looking from one of them to the other.

"He's going to be all right, I hope."

Connie opened both eyes wide. Behind them in the hall was somebody else. For an instant she didn't recognize him. Then she remembered. "Oh, Mr. Vanaman," she said. "What are you—"

"The forgotten man," Gus murmured. He reached in his pocket for a cigarette. "What can we do for you, Vanaman?" he said.

Mr. Vanaman was doing all right for himself. He had taken Janey's hand and was shaking it with cordiality.

"This is a great pleasure, Mrs. Blake." Holding her hand still, he turned to Connie. His hawk eyes were sharp and bright. "I took the liberty of using your telephone to ask Mrs. Blake to come here and join Mr. Blake. It was . . . presumptuous. But I wanted to be the first to break the good news to her, and him, and to offer if needed my professional advice and services."

Janey looked blankly from him to Gus, and back again.

"I . . . I don't know what you're talking about, Mr. . . ."

"Vanaman, Mrs. Blake."

He dropped her hand. He drew a document from his inside coat pocket.

"You know, of course, Mrs. Blake, that your father was a great friend of my late client Paul M. Wernitz. There's no point in my going into details at this time, nor would it be proper for me to divulge all of them here. But Mr. Wernitz, who had no living relatives, did not forget his friendship with your father when I drew up his will for him. And what I want personally to be the first to tell you, Mrs. Blake: he also remembered you."

Her blue eyes opened wide. "He—"

"He remembered you, Mrs. Blake. I can't tell you how much personal pleasure it gives me to tell you that Mr. Wernitz has left to you all of his interest in the *Smithville Evening Gazette*. In fact, we may as well say the *Smithville Gazette* is yours. Ninety per cent of the stock certainly constitutes you owner and publisher."

He shook Janey's limp hand again.

"I hurried back from New York especially, in case some one else might give you the news instead of myself."

Mr. Vanaman looked beamingly around at the others. His smile, cordial and alive, quietly died, faded and disappeared. He looked from one to another in the dumbfounded silence.

"May I . . . is there . . . may I ask what is the matter with all of you?"

His eyes, darting rapidly, fixed themselves on Orvie Rogers.

"Is there anything funny in what I've said, Mr. Rogers? What *is* the matter?"

Orvie Rogers gulped and got his voice. "No," he said hastily. "Not at all. There's nothing at all the matter. It's not . . . it's not funny. It's wonderful. Nothing's the matter at all."

Gus Blake found his voice too. "Not a thing in the world, Vanaman," he said as easily as he could.

"Nothing at all, Mr. Vanaman," Connie Maynard said. She laughed suddenly. "Except . . . except that the editor of the *Smithville Gazette* is Mrs. Blake's husband. And he has prejudices. He won't work for a dame. He said so publicly this very evening." She laughed again.

Still Janey hadn't spoken. Mr. Vanaman smiled again, puzzled still but vaguely reassured. "Well. It wouldn't seem—"

Janey's blank uncomprehending face had begun gradually to light up. It broke out now into the old radiant delighted smile, her blue eyes shining as if all the stars in the Milky Way had suddenly collided and were shooting off a million splinters of light. She turned to Gus and started to go to him. He stood there propped against the high carved mantelpiece. Janey stopped, her lips parted. She caught her breath, swallowed, and turned back to Mr. Hugo Vanaman. She could feel the bright glow creeping along her pale cheeks as she went dizzily toward him.

"You've been very kind! I'll . . . I'll talk this over with my husband . . . he'll know better what we ought to do."

She looked at Gus again. "—If we went home now, maybe . . . maybe we could . . . could talk about this?"

Connie Maynard went toward the door. "It mightn't be a bad idea," she said, "if we leave the proprietors alone, for this scene. What about a drink, Mr. Vanaman? You and Orvie and I could probably find one in the pantry."

"Good," Orvie Rogers said. He smiled. He added, surprisingly, "I've always admired unexpected tact."

At the door Connie turned back. "I suppose," she said, "this means I don't have a job any more. Shall I quit, madame publisher, or would you rather have the pleasure of firing me?"

Janey's eyes widened. "Oh, no, Connie!" she said quickly. "I don't . . . I wouldn't want to be mean! I . . . I guess people are only mean when they're unhappy, and afraid. And I'm not either any more." She smiled at Connie, and at Gus. "Anyway, I don't have anything to do with that. That's the editor's job, not the publisher's. Except I do think you might do a . . . a spectacular and . . . different sort of Woman's Page. But right now I'd rather you'd use your . . . your waning influence to get the editor to come home. I'm still terribly in love with him."

She flashed her radiant springtime smile at both of them. Connie laughed again. "I'll brush up on my bran muffins in the morning." She looked over at Gus. "You heard what the Big Boss said."

"—Gus knows I don't want to be anybody's boss, Connie."

Gus Blake prodded himself out of his moon-struck trance and grinned as he moved away from the sustaining mantelpiece. He came over to her.

"I've taken that all back, Janey," he said very soberly. "I don't want to quit my job. There's one little dame I want to go on working for as long as she'll let me." He looked down at her through a blue twinkling mist. "So let's go home, Janey. I love you. I . . . I never knew how much until—"

"Oh, don't, Gus—please don't," she whispered quickly. "I understand. You don't have to—"

"Good girl."

He bent down and kissed her gently on the top of her small tow head.

THE END

www.ingramcontent.com/pod-product-compliance
Lightning Source LLC
Chambersburg PA
CBHW030335020726
47493CB00004B/1278